Volume Five

Airship 27 Productions

Dan Fowler: G-Man Volume Five

"In the Skin" and "Shine of the Moon" ©2025 Fred Adams Jr.

Edited by Ron Fortier
Associate Editor: Myles Robertson

Cover illustration ©2025 Michael Youngblood
Interior illustrations ©2025 Sam Salas
Production and design by Rob Davis
Marketing management by Michael Vance

Published by
Airship 27 Productions
www.airship27hangar.com

ISBN: 978-1-953589-95-8

Produced in the United States of America

10 9 8 7 6 5 4 3 2 1

Dan Fowler
G-Man
Volume Five

by
Fred Adams Jr.

TABLE OF CONTENTS

IN THE
SKIN

(1)

Tom Metzler looked into the wastebasket and cursed under his breath. Orange peels, coffee grounds, and what looked like a half bowl of vegetable soup someone had dumped into it. Pigs, he thought. He picked up the wastebasket and almost gagged. You'd think after seven years he'd be used to the stink. A thought crossed his mind. He tugged at the file drawer of the desk beside the trash can and it slid open; unlocked, with all those important papers. He lifted the wastebasket and tipped it to pour the slop onto the files but stopped short. He needed the job more than he needed the satisfaction.

Metzler found pushing a broom demeaning. Emptying the trash bins was worse. Cleaning the toilets was the bottom of the pile. Before the Crash, he'd been a master machinist for a cruise line, close to his pension. Then everything fell apart in one day. All gone.

The job was demeaning, but it was a job. At least he didn't spend his days in soup lines and his nights sleeping on park benches or in doorways. But he still had to root through garbage cans for his living. For nearly eight years he had worked as a "maintenance man," a fancy name for janitor at the Bureau of Engraving and Printing in D.C. He laughed bitterly at the irony. He used to have all the money he needed; now he mopped the floors where they printed it for everyone else.

He was moved to the Annex, the big, new tomb of a building across the street from the BEP when it opened in '39 and his workload doubled, but a job was a job, and he'd put up with it as long as he had to.

He dumped the wastebasket into the wheeled garbage can that he pushed around the floor all night and rolled it into the corridor. His footsteps echoed in the empty hallway, the only other sound the squeak of the wheels. Night shift made for bad sleeping, but he liked it better than the day turn. At night, there was nobody in a suit to snicker at him as he did his job. He opened the door to the next office, another room full of bureaucrat desks, and reached for the light switch.

A hand with a grip like a pair of pliers closed on his wrist, and he felt a pain from a heavy blow to his throat. His wind pipe collapsed, cutting off his air. His world turned upside down as he was lifted off his feet and tipped head down into the garbage can. His open mouth filled with the coffee grounds and orange peels. But it didn't matter anymore. Tom Metzler was dead.

5

In the Annex's next wing, Billy Krajovic mopped the terrazzo floor in the main hallway. He didn't mind the job so much. He got used to hard work in the coal mines of Western Pennsylvania. Then one Friday at noon, the company announced that the mines were closed, and the money bags walked away leaving the thousands of immigrant laborers stranded in their patch towns with nowhere to go and no way to get there.

He was one mouth too many for his family to feed, so the teenager drifted around for almost two years, camping in hobo jungles and sleeping under bridges until he came to Washington, D.C. It was sheer luck that put him in line for a janitor's job at the Bureau. Slinging a mop was nowhere near as hard as digging coal with a pick. And he was able to send a little money home to his family every few weeks. They were surviving; he was surviving, and in those times, little else mattered.

He looked down the dimly lit hall. Another fifty feet and this job would be done. He wrung his mop in the bucket, looked up again, and saw a man standing ten feet away. He was dressed in the same work greens Billy wore and had a cap perched over a shock of caramel colored hair.

"Hey Stroud. What's up?"

"Nothing with me. Now, the man behind you…"

Before Billy could turn, stars exploded in his head from a heavy blow. A hard hand grabbed a handful of Billy's hair behind his ear. The attacker kicked his feet from under him, and shoved his head into the mop bucket . Billy was strong, but in his dazed condition, he could offer little resistance. For a moment he flopped like a landed trout, arms and legs flailing, then he lay still.

Arthur Savage leaned back in the chair at the head of the big walnut table where the upper–ups met and conferred. He flicked an ash from his cigarette into the cut glass ashtray. Stroud had put him onto the brand, and he was glad. A Turkish Elite, and it tasted like heaven after years of smoking cheap cigarettes that were half horseshit or picking butts out of the bigwigs' ashtrays. They cost like caviar, but everybody needs to indulge himself once in a while.

Four years he'd been working in the Annex, cleaning, polishing, shining, making the big shots' offices look and feel regal, because that's what they thought they were, a kind of royalty. They made him want to puke, walking around with their noses in the air. Bastards, treating us all like slaves, he thought. He turned at a sound behind him and saw Stroud standing in the doorway. Stroud jerked his head, and Savage threw his dust rag on the table, stubbed out his cigarette and followed him through the anteroom, where he stepped over the corpse of a uniformed guard.

Another man, one the size of an icebox in a set of work greens, was waiting in the hallway. To the big man Savage said, "This way, Tuds," and started for the elevator with his companions in tow.

Three floors down in the basement of the building, Savage stepped off the elevator with Tuds. A uniformed guard rose from his desk. "Hello, Savage. Who's this?"

"New night man, Willy. I'm taking him around for introductions and then teaching him the routine."

Willy picked up a clipboard and scanned the top sheet. "I don't see anything about it on the dailies."

Savage pulled a folded sheet of paper from his pocket and offered it to Willy. "Bureaucracy. Here's the order."

Willy stepped from behind his desk and between the men to retrieve it. When he did, Tuds grabbed his head in both hands and wrenched it with a sound like twisting a crisp stalk of celery. Savage took Willy's gun and his keys and they hid his body in the foot well of the desk. The elevator door opened and Stroud stepped out.

"Three down, one to go."

(2)

"Good morning, Ira." Dan Fowler laid a dollar bill on the newsstand counter. "Hi, Mister Fowler," the little man behind the counter said, reaching for a stack of papers. "Here you go." He laid out three dailies, the Washington Post, the New York Times, and the Pittsburgh Press.

Fowler scooped up the papers and said, "Keep the change, Ira." He tucked the papers under his arm and looked at his watch; plenty of time for breakfast before he went to the office.

He crossed the street and turned up 10th Street Northwest. The July sun was bright but not hot enough yet to make honest people sweat.

Fowler was the sort of man the average person might call imposing if not intimidating. Standing six feet four inches, his two hundred pounds of bone and muscle carried a head with a face that belied his age. The lines around his eyes and his craggy features made him appear older than his thirty–two years. His broad–shouldered, slim–hipped build filled his tan suit in a way that turned women's heads as he walked by.

Four blocks from the Bureau offices, Fowler went into Morrie's, a diner tucked between a haberdashery and a cinema. He slid into a booth and before he could open his newspapers, Marge, the waitress scurried over with a cup and saucer in one hand, and a coffee pot in the other. "What'll you have today, Mister Fowler?"

"Eggs over easy with bacon and toast, and a glass of tomato juice."

"I didn't even have to write it down," she said with a laugh, putting her pad and pencil in the pocket of her uniform. "You order the same thing every time."

"Someday, I'll surprise you, Marge."

She laughed and tucked her pencil behind an ear. "On the way."

He opened the Times first and scanned the front page. He always read the Times first, the Press for a second opinion, and finally the Post for the political slant. The big news was from across the pond. Prime Minister Neville Chamberlain basically told his Japanese counterpart Fuminaro Konoe "nuts" to the Japanese demand that the Brits reverse their foreign policy in the Far East and leave China ripe for conquest. The FBI's operations were strictly stateside, and Fowler was more interested in what was happening in the U.S., particularly the Underworld, but he liked to keep up with current events.

Marge brought his platter and refilled his coffee. Fowler continued to read as he ate. A second bank robbery in Kansas in two weeks. Putting Ben and Stella Dixon behind bars didn't seem to have slowed the trade much, he thought, but that was a matter for the KC field office unless they got a line on a fugitive, then the phone on his desk would ring.

Dan Fowler was a Special Investigator, a manhunter who served at the pleasure of the Director. He could be called upon day or night to travel anywhere in the country to track down the worst of the worst.

As the Director put it, Fowler had "a nose for evil," and his record for apprehension rivaled the best of the Bureau. His successes had put him on the fast track for promotion and made him the youngest man in the Bureau to be promoted to that rank, to the admiration of some, and the jealous dislike of others.

Fowler was on his second piece of toast when the diner door opened and a tall, trim man in a suit came in. It was fellow agent Bob Martin. He scanned the patrons and spotted Fowler, who spotted him at the same time. When the newcomer didn't slide into the booth, Fowler knew he wouldn't be finishing his breakfast.

"Don't tell me," Fowler said.

"The Director needs you. He said, 'Now.'"

Fowler downed the last of his juice, folded his newspapers, and left a two dollar bill under his coffee cup. "Let's go." As they walked toward Pennsylvania Avenue, Fowler asked, "Any idea what this is all about?"

"Not a clue. But the Director is pretty hot about something."

"I guess I'll find out soon enough."

In moments they were climbing the steps of the Department of Justice Building, home to the Bureau's offices and the office of the Director. Three floors up, Fowler left Martin and walked down the long hallway to the door of his own office with INSPECTOR DANIEL FOWLER in black letters on the pebbled glass. He opened the door and threw the newspapers on the desk then hung his fedora on the coat tree, straightened his necktie and headed to see the Director.

The Director was his usual dyspeptic self, but when your job is protecting 130 million American citizens from the other .9 million, it not only came with the turf, it was the turf. "Close the door, Agent Fowler." He did. The Director never used last names only when addressing his people; he always acknowledged rank. Fowler suspected it was less a matter of respect than his way of reminding them of their rung on the ladder.

He stood to the side of his desk looking out the window at the bustle below on Pennsylvania Avenue. "Look down there. To know what's going on in this country, all I have to do is look out this window. Five years ago, you didn't see all that traffic. People couldn't afford cars, or if they owned one, they couldn't afford gasoline or tires. The economy is recovering. Roosevelt says so every time he's on the radio. It's coming back, but it's fragile."

The Director opened the main drawer of his enormous desk and pulled out something large and flat wrapped in newspaper. He set it on the desk with a clank and peeled back the wrapping from a corner of the package. "You know what these are?"

Fowler immediately recognized a pair of twelve–to–a–sheet printing plates, front and back for twenty dollar bills. The steel gleamed in the sunlight streaming through the window blinds. On each of the sheets, the lower right hand corner was missing.

"Looks like somebody got ambitious with a hacksaw."

The Director snorted. "When the Treasury Department went from eight bills per sheet to twelve, they thought the plates would be more difficult to steal. They didn't count on criminal ingenuity."

"For every man who makes a lock, there's someone who can make a key, sir. When did this happen?"

"Eight hours ago at the BEP Annex. Guards at the shift change found three dead guards and those." He nodded at the plates.

"But it would take a lot of work to print up a significant amount of money one bill at a time unless he just did up a few twenties every week to pay for groceries. And the thief would need access to the right paper."

"Just bleach a dozen dollar bills and you've got the paper. The Treasury Department's concern is that the plate can be duplicated and the country would be flooded with bogus money."

"Whoever did this was pretty smart. If he stole plates for a fifty or a C–note, the bills would attract attention. Who carries hundreds in his wallet besides the Rockefellers? Most businesses could change a twenty these days and never think twice about it."

"That's true. The real worry is what could happen to economic recovery if word got out. It's the faith in our currency that keeps the whole house of cards standing. "

"Any leads?"

"Four janitors, of all people. All four were on shift last night and all four are missing this morning. None of them has a record, but one of them, Arthur

Savage, used to be a big wheel on Wall Street before the Crash. Start with him. The President wants us to take the lead on this, Treasury doesn't like it, but orders are orders. Your liaison with Treasury is an agent named Ennis Cooper."

"I'll go to see him now. What's his pedigree?"

The Director snorted. "He's a grade A pencil pusher. His investigative experience is mainly in Forensic Accounting."

"It brought down Capone when we couldn't get him any other way."

The Director frowned. "Don't remind me. Cooper's waiting outside. And Fowler,"

"Sir?"

"This has to be absolutely hush-hush, the President's orders. He doesn't want another Wall Street panic. I'd rather leave Treasury out of it too, but this mess started in their backyard. I'd like to put the whole Bureau on it, but we can't risk leaks. For now, it'll be just you and Kendall."

"Yes, sir."

The Director turned his back to look out the window. Dismissed.

(3)

Ennis Cooper had a pinched look to his face that reminded Fowler of the husband in Grant Wood's American Gothic coupled with the resigned stoicism of the wife. He was dressed in what Fowler thought of as "the uniform": dark blue pinstriped suit, starched white shirt, dark necktie and Oxfords polished to a high gloss. He might as well wear his badge on his breast pocket, Fowler thought.

What's the word his grandmother used to tag stuffed shirts?

Pecksniff.

That was the word.

"You're Cooper?"

Cooper nodded and stood to shake Fowler's hand.

"Let's not waste time," Fowler said. "I need to see the crime scene before the trail goes cold."

"Nothing's been disturbed," Cooper said.

"Good. Let's get over there."

On the way, Cooper told Fowler that during the night, the thieves had murdered three guards and opened the vault in which currency printing plates were kept. "They short circuited the alarm system between the start of one shift and the start of the next. They knew what they were doing, no doubt about it."

"Tell me about the janitors," Fowler said.

"They were all cleared and worked in the old building for years. When the operation moved into the Annex, they were part of the existing crew who were brought across the street." He shook his head. "Janitors. Who would have guessed?"

"You think they were the insiders?"

Cooper nodded. "I have nothing to do with personnel, so I never had any contact with Savage, Stroud, Krajovic, or Metzler. But looking at their files, I found out that a few of them are pretty sharp. One of them was an Ivy Leaguer."

"Savage?"

"No, James Stroud. Two years at Yale before the Depression hit."

"But Savage was the Wall Street vest."

"Yes. He was a Wharton grad. Stroud never had the chance at a career, unless you count pushing a broom. The odd two are Krajovic and Metzler. Krajovic has no education past the sixth grade, no previous work experience that didn't involve a pick or shovel; not exactly a criminal mastermind."

"Maybe they needed muscle, or he had the keys they didn't. Or maybe he tumbled to what they were doing and they had to include him."

"Metzler, was a machinist before the Crash."

"Technical know-how. The safe. Makes sense."

Well, all we know is they punched in last night and now they're gone without a trace. At this moment, they're all we've got."

"But there has to be somebody bigger behind it all. Four janitors couldn't operate a counterfeiting ring on their own scratch."

"Unless they plan to sell the plates, say to the highest bidder. Either way, it's a potential disaster if we don't get them back."

"You have photos of these guys?"

Cooper nodded. "I'll get you copies."

"The Annex has tunnels under the street, right?"

"One that connects it to the original building and one under D Street to the freight yards for rail shipments. Both guarded night and day, and no sign of activity."

They turned a corner, and the Annex came into view.

The Bureau of Engraving and Printing Annex across the street from the BEP had been occupied for less than a year, and every time he passed it, Fowler wondered why it was built the way it was. The Treasury Department boasted that it was the largest reinforced concrete structure in the world, at 523 feet long and 251 feet wide. Ten vertical wings were arranged in opposing pairs, alternated with low level building sections, making it look like a double rank of rectangular silos.

"So, did these four work together?"

"Each of them worked a separate section of the building."

"Do you know whether they palled around together after hours?"

"Not that anybody's ever seen, and we asked everybody in the building."

Cooper badged them past a pair of guards standing at port arms with riot guns.

"Are they always there?"

"No," he said, and offered no further explanation. Fowler followed him to a set of elevators that took them to the building's basement. When the doors opened downstairs, Fowler saw a bustle of uniforms and suits up and down the corridor. "This way."

They came to a barred gateway that led to a walk–in vault. The door gaped open and inside, men were taking photos and dusting for fingerprints. Two bodies lay covered with tarps.

"There's Al Manning, our lead investigator." Cooper pointed to a tall, heavy set man giving orders to a pair of fingerprint men.

"I'll meet him later. I think I'd just be in the way here. Take me around to see where the janitors were working when all this went down. I figure your guys will do a thorough job everywhere there's a bloodstain. I'd like to get a feel for the building and how these four fit in the picture."

Cooper looked annoyed at the order but didn't argue. "Very well. Follow me."

In the second wing, Cooper led Fowler to the third floor. The floor was quiet; people were going about their business, but talking in whispers. "How many know?" Fowler said.

"Almost nobody, and it has everyone spooked. They all know something big has happened, but they don't know what it is. Savage was working this floor. His trash maintenance cart is missing, but the last office he cleaned was that one." Cooper pointed to an open doorway where a uniformed guard barred the entrance. "There's trash in the wastebaskets of the rest of the rooms."

"Your men searched this floor?"

"Of course, and every inch of the wings where the four of them were work-ing. We aren't exactly rubes, Fowler."

"No offense intended, Cooper. Just gathering information. How many peo-ple total were in the building last night?"

"Between guards and maintenance, twenty-seven."

"Three guards killed?"

Cooper nodded. "None shot. All killed quietly; knife, garrotte, broken neck."

"No gunshot noise to attract attention. So whoever killed the guards was able to get close. The dead guards knew their killers."

"Another finger pointed at the janitors."

"And all this happened while other staff were in the building," Fowler mused. "That took a lot of planning."

"And inside knowledge."

"And balls."

Next was the conference room where Savage had been cleaning. A dust rag lay on the huge mahogany table beside a cut glass ashtray, one of three.

"He was waiting here for someone," Fowler said, "taking it easy."

"How can you know that?"

"Heel marks on that shiny table. And that." A single cigarette butt was crushed out in the one beside the rag. The others were clean and empty. Fowler leaned in close and studied the cigarette. "It's only been smoked halfway.

Somebody quit in the middle. And that's a waste."

Cooper's eyes narrowed. "A waste?"

"Are you a smoker?"

"Certainly not."

"See the three gold rings and the crown near the end? It's a Turkish Elite. Top tobacco and almost as expensive as a good cigar. Buck a pack. Not exactly suited to a janitor's salary. You may want to find out who if any of the people who have access to this room smoke these and whether they were in the building last night." Cooper opened his mouth to say something about Fowler telling him how to do his job but changed his mind.

In the next wing the hallway where Krajovic had been mopping had little to offer. The mop and bucket stood in a corner of the corridor. "It looks as if he stopped mopping here," Fowler said. "He was doing a sloppy job, too. There's a patch of dried soap scum over there."

"Like he quit in the middle of the job," said Cooper, "but why bother putting the mop in the bucket and rolling it away?"

"Who knows the criminal mind?"

"Excuse me, Agent Cooper." A uniformed guard stood at the head of the stairs. "We found Metzler's trash can. He's in it head down."

In the sub-basement of the Annex, a group of agents and officers stood around the wheeled garbage can with feet shod in black work brogans sticking out of the top. Manning saw Cooper and started over.

"What've you got here?"

The detective said, "We found the garbage can like you see it in that broom closet. Wallet in the hip pocket has an expired driver's license belongs to Tom Metzler."

"How did he die?" Fowler asked. Manning eyed him up and down.

"This is Special Agent Fowler," Cooper explained.

"Don't know yet. We haven't pulled him out. Waiting for the camera man."

"I suppose we can eliminate him as a suspect," Cooper said.

"Maybe. Maybe not," Fowler said. "They might have double crossed him once he served his purpose."

"We also found Savage's maintenance cart. Gives us a pretty good idea how they got around the building without being noticed. And we think we've figured out how they got away. Follow me."

At the end of a long hallway, a two-by-two steel plate painted to match the walls lay on the floor. Through the opening it had covered, Fowler saw closely packed pipes receding into darkness.

"That's the pipe chase across the street to the steam plant at the old building," Manning said. "Eight months out of the year, the heat's so bad a man couldn't survive in there long enough to cross the street. But it's shut down for the summer. Eight bolts and a lock, and Maintenance kept the key hanging on the rack in the office. It was bolted to keep people out. I guess nobody thought about keeping people in."

Manning kicked a bolt as thick as his thumb and it skittered across the concrete floor. He picked up another and held it between his thumb and forefinger. "The original bolts were three inches long. They've been replaced with these half-inchers."

"Metzler the machinist," Fowler said. "Saves time opening the chase."

Cooper broke in. "Dust them for prints, but I doubt we'll find any surprises."

Manning's face flushed at the unspoken condescension. "We have men going through the chase now. We don't expect to find any there, either, but we have to check."

"Is the pipe chase capped the same way at the other end?"

Cooper nodded. "But there are three vents along the way, again, built to keep people out, not in."

Fowler looked into the opening. "When you think about it, who better than a gang of janitors to pull this off? The guard staff saw them every day, and if one of them came wheeling his trash can down a corridor, no one would think that he's got a pair of stolen printing plates under the papers and the garbage."

"And who would think twice to see him roll near the vault area?" Cooper said. "It's the perfect disguise. But I agree there has to be a bigger partner in this, someone who enlisted the broom pushers to take advantage of the new building."

"I'd say this plot has been in the works for a long time."

"I agree."

"I've seen as much as I'm going to for now. If you'll get me those photos, I'll start on my legwork." Cooper disappeared for a few minutes, leaving Fowler alone with Manning.

"I don't mind telling you Fowler, there's some resentment in Treasury about the Bureau taking the lead on this case."

"Does that include you, Al?"

"Willie Sanger, one of the dead guards was a pal of mine. I want the animals who did this. I want them bad."

"So do I, Al. This arrangement came from way over my head. But when we catch them, and we will, I can promise you a ringside seat at the execution. Just remember, we're all on the same team here."

"Maybe they'll let me throw the switch on Old Sparky."

Cooper returned shortly with a manila folder. "Here are the pictures from their personnel files. One of the guards said that Savage grew a mustache a few months ago."

Fowler handed Cooper a card. "Keep me posted. The first number is my office. The second is the main switchboard at the Bureau if you have a message to leave."

Cooper nodded and handed Fowler a card of his own. "Ditto."

Fowler walked out the front doors of the Annex into the bright sunshine, past the guards who paid him no mind. They were busy doing their job, keeping people out, not keeping them in. He reached into his pocket and pulled out the cigarette he'd pocketed in the conference room. Turkish Elites; pricey for a janitor, unless of course the janitor was moonlighting for a mobster.

(4)

His next stop was Pipe Dreams, the tobacconist three blocks from his office. Art Miller, the owner could tell him who else in the capital sold Turkish Elites and who bought them from him.

Pipe Dreams was a cozy shop, a quiet haven in the bustling city where a man could buy a good cigar and enjoy it in the smoker's lounge to the rear, the way a businessman might have a martini with lunch. Fowler bought cigars from Miller from time to time and knew he would be cooperative. A plus: Congressmen, Senators, lobbyists, and even some of the city's top criminals patronized the place, so Art was a source of tantalizing bits of information overheard between puffs.

The spring bell rang as Fowler opened the door and stepped out of the sidewalk heat. The aroma of fine tobacco was almost intoxicating. Art was behind the glass–fronted display counter unpacking a small wooden crate. "Hi, Dan." He held up a cigar. "You should try one of these. Romeo y Julietta. Just came in from Cuba."

"No thanks, Art. Not today. I'm trying to get a line on these." He pointed through the glass to a rank of cigarette tins, red enameled with three rings and a crown and the words TURKISH ELITE in gold.

"You get a raise or something?" Miller grinned. "Those are really pricey."

"What I'm really interested in is who might have smoked this one." Fowler held the butt between his thumb and forefinger.

Art raised an eyebrow. "A case?"

"A big one." He reached into his pocket and laid out the photos of the three janitors on the counter. Ever see any of these men?"

"Him." Miller immediately put a finger on Stroud's photo. "He comes in here once in a while. Has a smoke in the back room, usually a cigar. Never saw him in this outfit, though. He's a pretty sharp dresser."

"You know his name?"

Miller shook his head. "No need. He pays cash and he's never special ordered anything."

"Has he ever bought Turkish Elites?"

Art nodded. "He started coming in here about a year ago. I figured him for a money belt by his clothes and his taste in tobacco. Who is he?"

"A janitor."

Art's eyebrows raised. "Oh yeah? Maybe I'm in the wrong business."

"Maybe he just likes to put on airs."

"Well, let me tell you, Dan. He keeps some interesting company. You know Ciggy Signorelli. He comes in here regular, and plenty of times I've seen him sitting in the Smoke Room talking head to head with your pal here like a pair of Bolsheviks."

"Signorelli The Collector?'

"The same."

"You wouldn't have happened to hear what they were talking about, would you?"

"Every once in a while I'd hear a bit, but it was all in Italian. I'm a Johnny Bull from end to end."

Fowler nodded. "I see. Well, thanks for the tip, Art. I don't have to tell you this conversation is on the Q.T."

Miller made a buttoning pantomime on his lower lip.

"And, I think I'll try one of those Romeo y Juliettas."

Art handed one to him. "Shall I cut it for you?"

"No thanks. I'll take it with me. He reached for his money clip. What do I owe you?"

"Ten bucks."

Fowler laid a bill on the counter without blinking. "Thanks, Art. I'll see you soon." Fowler walked out of the shop turning the cigar in his fingers. He'd turn in the whole ten as snitch pay and have a good smoke besides.

More puzzles. So the cigarette wasn't left by some outsider. A rich janitor with mob associates. Stroud looked better for the caper all the time. But what about the other two? What role did they play? And Signorelli, the sadistic collection agent for loan shark Tito Marcoletto. Fowler never knew him to pass funny money. Was the gang branching out? In the words of Alice, "curiouser and curiouser."

(5)

"How long Doc?" Stroud said.

Doctor Macon rinsed his hands in the sink, the water going down the drain turning from red to pink to clear. He cupped a double handful of cold water and splashed it in his face. "At least a week. I told your boss that. He has to be watched to make sure there's no infection. They won't let him on the ship if he's got a fever. And I've never embedded something so large before, let alone a double job."

The man on the table was out cold and breathing steadily. Macon opened his bag and pulled out a pint of gin. He tipped the bottle back and took a long pull.

Stroud frowned. "No sooner, huh?" He was antsy to get things moving because he wouldn't get paid until Pouch was on his way to Europe. Stroud wanted to get his money and get away. By now, the Feds were running full tilt looking for Savage and for him. Every day he had to babysit was one more day he might get caught. All he wanted to do was get Pouch in the car, drive to Boston, and put him on the Bella Maria for Italy. Marcoletto promised him a cool twenty grand on delivery, and Stroud was already spending the cash in his head.

He was about to light a cigarette when Macon put up a restraining hand. "Not in here. You want to smoke, take it outside. This is a surgery, not a nightclub."

The nerve of that rummy, Stroud thought. He wanted to punch the doc in the teeth, but he didn't want to upset the cart. Doc Macon was part of the Organization. At this point, Stroud was only hired help. He stepped out onto the porch of the hunting lodge and breathed in the fresh smell of the mountain pines, not too different from the antiseptic smell indoors. Marcoletto chose the place because it was the remotest county in the Commonwealth. Ten minutes and you'd be in Kentucky and out the reach of the Virginia State Police if things got hot.

Locals called the place The Dark Forest, and it made Stroud uncomfortable. The cabin was hidden in a dense growth of oaks and maple trees that grew so close together that if you chopped away the roots of one you'd have to chop down the three or four around it so the first one could fall. Fifty feet away you couldn't see the cabin anymore. A hundred feet away and you might not find it again without a compass.

Stroud was a city boy, and the quiet bothered him. He was used to the undercurrent of city sounds, the taxis, the streetcars, the garbage trucks. And what bothered him at least as much were the sounds of the woods at night; the rustling, the occasional snarl or growl, and the eerie cry of the night birds.

Beyond the end of civilization, the cabin nestled in a hollow between two spines of the Appalachian range. The nearest town was ten miles south on dirt roads and cow paths. And he was going to be here for a week. No phone. He counted the cigarettes in the case and stubbed out his smoke half done. That was one thing he didn't think about, enough cigarettes to last him. Maybe when Marcoletto's boys came to check on them, they could get him some. He knew the hick town's general store wouldn't have Turkish Elites, but they might at least have Chesterfields.

It would be a long week. He hoped the lodge had a deck of cards. And Stroud hoped his charge knew how to play Fan Tan. He rubbed his chin. He needed a shave. Betty would be coming soon and she wouldn't want to go to work with beard burn on her jugs —the hazards of dating a stripper.

The man on the table was Tommy Barstow. He had plenty of nicknames; Tommy Barstool, Tommy Tiptoe and the most important, more like a code name or secret identity than a nickname: Pouch. That was mobster Tito Marcoletto's tag for the courier. Marcoletto gave everybody a nickname. It made him feel superior to the rest of mugs in his world.

Barstow was recruited, shanghaied if you will, from a life of private criminal enterprise by Marcoletto's gang because of his special abilities. He was a smuggler, diamonds and precious gems mostly. Maybe abilities wasn't the best word.

Once, Tommy had been fat; more than fat, grossly obese, and then he lost a lot of weight. When you blow up like he did then lose all the excess baggage, your skin hangs on you like socks on a rooster. Flaps, folds, and sagging inner tubes. All those pockets and tucks, all those places to hide things; subcutaneous, the docs called it, under the skin. But Tommy's real gift was a high tolerance for discomfort.

One doctor would open him up and put the contraband inside him then sew him up again. Wait a week or two 'til the stitches were out, and he'd walk through Customs like the Apostle Paul. Then at his destination, another sawbones would open him up and retrieve the swag. Tommy was a literal bag man. He'd been lucky so far. Then his luck ran out, maybe. Or maybe not.

He was doing all right for a couple of years; maybe make a run every six months, get paid in cash, and live high for a while, then when the money ran low, make a few calls, and head for Amsterdam, Paris, Mexico City, and in a month, back to the old U. S. of A. That was before Tito decided to send his boys to bring Tommy to him.

Tommy had been back in country for three days after bringing in a half million dollars in cut diamonds under his left kidney. The difference between the States and Switzerland was heads and tails. In Switzerland, he was checked into a private sanatorium in the mountains north of Bern. In New York, he was taken to a clinic in a crummy neighborhood where a doc two whiskeys away from DTs took out the diamonds and cut him loose in two hours. He camped out at his apartment to convalesce and just as he was beginning to feel normal again, the knock came.

Three of them, all hard-eyed muscle.

"Someone wants to talk to you, Barstow. Come with us." No badges. No invitation. No argument.

One drove, and the other two bookended him in the back seat. The ride was short, and they didn't bother blindfolding him or making him hide on the floor of the big blue Oldsmobile sedan. They didn't care if he knew where they were taking him. That could be good, or it could be bad. The car pulled up in front of the entrance to the Blue Bunny Club on 54th. Everybody got out and they frog marched him through the front doors, through the foyer, and onto the main floor.

A nightclub is eerie in the middle of the afternoon. The only lights shine from odd places behind the bar, offstage, or from open doorways, casting stark shadows. A room that was full of music, laughter and popping corks twelve hours before now lay silent. Their footsteps echoed as the goons took Tommy by the elbows to a far corner of the show floor where a shadowy figure sat alone in a three-quarter booth.

"Bring our guest a chair," he said. The voice had an ironic, sneering quality to it, as if the speaker were snickering over a dirty joke.

A chair scraped up behind Tommy's legs, and rough hands pushed him into the seat.

Tommy winced, and the shadow said. "Easy, boys. Tommy just had surgery. Isn't that right, Tommy?"

No answer. No one spoke for almost a minute.

"You don't talk about it. I like that." A lighter flicked, and in its flame, Tommy saw the owner of the voice. The lean face with its pointed chin, long nose and knife scar at the corner of his left eye. Tito Marcoletto. The mobster lit a cigarette and took a long drag before he snapped the Zippo shut. "You know who I am?"

"Everybody knows who you are."

"I guess so." Tito laughed. "I ain't much for small talk. I got a job for you, Tommy. You'll do it."

(6)

Back in his office, Fowler sat at his desk jotting down names, facts, and ideas. Across the desk, the handsome Agent Larry Kendall, Fowler's partner and friend, wrote notes of his own. The personnel files on Stroud, Savage, and Krajovic that Cooper had sent over lay open on the desk between them.

"How's our liaison in Treasury?"

"Cooper's a nebbish. He wants to be in the middle of things, and he'd only be in the way. I'd rather work with their Chief Investigator, Manning, but it's Treasury's call. By the way, the Director doesn't think much of Cooper either."

"So," Kendall said, changing the subject, "we're focusing on this Stroud guy?"

"But not excluding the other two. This is obviously an inside job, and it seems too complicated for just one man."

Kendall tapped a pencil against his perfect upper teeth. "In some ways the plot is brilliant, but in some ways it makes no sense. I could understand swiping twelve-bill plates. Why cut out one bill? A counterfeiting operation would be better served with full plates. And who would want the plates but counterfeiters?"

"I agree it's a twisted skein. We're missing something subtle here. We need to back up and see all around it. Cooper's men have already been to the residences of these three looking for them. No sign of any of the broom pushers. But we should take a close look at their rooms ourselves."

"I agree." Kendall shook out a Lucky from the pack. "My money would have been on Savage, "but this business with Stroud and Signorelli has me puzzled. Why would a loan shark like Tito Marcoletto suddenly jump into counterfeiting?"

Fowler sat at his desk jotting down names, facts, and ideas.

"Maybe it's just opportunity." Fowler rubbed his eyes with his thumbs. "Maybe one, or all of them are into Marcoletto for money and he dangled a chance at a clean slate if they played along."

"It's not like it hasn't happened before," Larry said. "Other places, other faces."

"Keep digging. I'm going to go pay a visit to Byron Clipp. If anyone knows the ins and outs of the game, it's he."

Larry chuckled. "Polishing up your speech, huh? 'He,' not 'him.' The Director'll be proud of you. Isn't Clipp's parole finished?"

Fowler nodded. "Almost. He's still in town. Has a job with Steinmetz Jewelry as an engraver. It was a condition of his parole, and he decided that he liked it. He knows he can't go back to his old career. The Law will be watching him close for the rest of his days. So instead, he works as an unofficial 'consultant' for the Bureau to polish apples for his parole officer." Fowler pushed back his chair. He stood and stretched and put on his hat. "Time to beat the bushes."

Some agents pored over files and dossiers for hours. Fowler, with his remarkable memory had little need for the paper trail. He knew more than the files contained in most cases, and he could recall the information with ease. Whom to talk to, and where to find them ran through his mind, and he had settled on Byron Clipp as his next step. But first, a quick walk downstairs.

Sally Vane sat at her desk, typing with the speed of a Tommy gun. She looked up as Fowler came through the doorway into her office and gave him a broad smile. He crossed to her desk and sat on a corner. "Busy day?"

"Every day." She stopped typing and brushed a damp strand of wavy blond hair away from her forehead. "Did you order this heat?"

Fowler laughed. "Sure did. Good for the corn crop."

"Well maybe you can scale it back a little tomorrow."

"Still doing your own typing, huh?" Despite being one of the first women accepted as an agent by the Bureau, Sally still did much of her own clerical work.

"Someday, I'll have a secretary, just like the boys. In the meantime, I can type faster than most of the girls in the Typing Pool, anyway." Sally changed the subject. "You asked about my day. How's yours?"

"Just as busy." He looked over his shoulder at the open door. "Can't talk about it here and now. Maybe tonight over dinner? I'd be delighted if you'd join me."

Sally rolled her eyes. "Maybe. I Bet you say that to all the typists."

"Only the pretty ones."

She swatted at him with an open hand. "Go do your duty, Dan."

He put two fingers to his forehead in a mock salute. "Will do, boss."

Her expression turned from playful to serious. "And please, be careful."

"Always, Sally." He wanted to lean over and kiss her, but fraternization between Bureau employees was frowned upon, and displays of affection taboo. The whole Bureau knew the two were an item, but let it go with a wink and a nod. "I'll call you later." He had to settle for pinching her cheek and headed for the door. He had to remind himself that despite her feminine beauty, Sally was an agent and was thoroughly trained in firearms and self–defense. In a tight spot, she was as capable and dangerous as any man. Dinner with Sally was a pleasure on its own dime, but tonight he wanted to run the case past her and get a different perspective.

(7)

Fowler grabbed a quick sandwich in a nearby automat and headed back to headquarters. Outside, the afternoon heat was becoming oppressive. Fowler felt the sweat trickle down his back as he walked up the street toward the Bureau garage where a car was waiting. His coupe was still in the shop having bullet holes patched from an encounter with kidnappers. Smiley, the Motor Pool chief saw him coming and pulled a set of keys from a hook board behind his desk. "It's your lucky day, Fowler," he said, handing the keys to the agent.

Fowler studied the ignition key. Its head was a crown over a shield with a coat of arms. "Cadillac, huh? How do I rate?"

"'Hobson's choice', Fowler. It's next in line. It was confiscated in a raid on Johnny Marcolini's Casino in Chevy Chase, and now we have it. It's in twenty–three." He jerked his thumb down the ranks of cars and trucks that lined the walls of the garage. He passed flivvers, coupes, a stake side farm truck, a mail truck with a right hand steering wheel, a Checker cab, and even a heavy duty tandem Chevy truck with a wedge shaped battering ram across its grille, a relic from the days of Prohibition. Its nickname was the Rammer.

The car in space twenty-three made Fowler's eyebrows rise. It wasn't just a Cadillac, it was a 1936 Series 60 roadster. The cream paint job glowed in the harsh overhead lights. The top was up, but through the windshield, Fowler saw the brown leather interior. Twin in-fender spare tires, gleaming wheel covers, Egyptian white walls, and the chromed "flying goddess" hood ornament gave the car an extra measure of class. The sleek design radiated poise, confidence, and speed, and the Caddy seemed to look you in the eye and say, "Up yours, Mac."

"A beauty, ain't she?" Fowler turned and saw Benny, the head grease monkey standing behind him.

"Sure is. What's she got, a V-8?"

"Three hundred twenty-two cubes worth. A hundred twenty-five brute horses. She'll do ninety and a little more, no sweat." Benny reached under the prow of the hood and pulled the catch. He raised the hood to show Fowler a hefty L-head V-8 engine. "I tuned this baby myself."

"I'll drive it as if it were my own."

Benny laughed. "Yeah, that's what I'm afraid of. I've seen a few of the cars you've used when they were towed in here, or on a flatbed in sections."

"Don't worry, Benny. I'll drive it with kid gloves. Give me a hand with the top, will you. I want to work on my suntan."

Benny shut the hood and undid the catches that held the rag top to the windshield frame. In a minute it was stowed and covered with a white canvas tonneau. Fowler opened the driver's door, one foot on the wide running board. With the top down, he could see the hump of the rear deck and the handle to open the rumble seat. Not a bad looking car. Fowler slid under the steering wheel. Benny leaned into the window. "Reach under the dash right below the speedometer. You'll feel a petcock."

Fowler felt under the dashboard and his fingers closed on a T-valve. "What's it do?"

"It opens the line to an auxiliary fuel tank in case Johnny M ran low on gas while he was running from the law —or his competitors. The filler is under the step plate for the rumble seat."

"Handy, but I doubt I'll need it. Plenty of gas stations along the way."

"If you have the time to stop."

Fowler slid the key into the ignition and pushed the starter button. The engine turned over in seconds, quiet, even, precise; no knocks, no shuddering, but Fowler could feel the power through his foot on the clutch, like a horse straining at the bit. He gave Benny a nod, and worked the shifter. The gears were like butter, and the roadster rolled out the door and into the street like a gliding falcon.

Four blocks from the garage, Fowler parked on a side street and went into a phone booth. He dropped in a nickel and dialed The Bureau. The switchboard connected him with the typing pool and Sally's desk.

"Pick you up at your place at six?"

"Sure. Where are we going?"

"Dinner. Out of town. I thought it would be a nice evening for a drive."

"I thought your car was in the shop having bullet holes filled in."

"I'll get one from the Motor Pool."

Fowler could almost see Sally's eyes roll through the telephone. "One of those ugly green sedans, I'll bet."

He decided to let the roadster be a surprise. "Hey, hon, 'Hobson's Choice'. You take what you get or nothing at all."

"I suppose I can hold my nose and hope none of my friends sees me in one of those old beat up Pontiacs."

Fowler laughed and looked through the glass of the booth at the roadster parked at the curb. "I'm sure you'll get through it somehow." He rang off and mopped his forehead with a handkerchief. The inside of the booth was like a greenhouse in the afternoon sun. He dropped another nickel and made reservations for six–thirty at the Blue Flame steakhouse across the border in Silver

Spring, one of Sally's favorite restaurants.

A third call went to Cooper. The switchboard at Treasury said he wasn't in and took the message. Fowler hung up the phone and stepped out of the booth before he had to wring out his suit.

(8)

Back in the car, he nosed into the gathering traffic and headed uptown. Steinmetz Jewelers was one of the foremost jewelry stores in the metropolitan D.C. area, featuring top quality merchandise and prices to match.

Striped canvas awnings kept the harsh glare of the sun away from the sidewalk windows, but they did little to dim the sparkle of the diamonds and polished gold of the necklaces, bracelets, and watches on display. Inside, the young woman behind the counter must have been new. She was charming to the point of flirtation until Fowler showed his badge. Her face tightened and she went for the owner.

Gerhard Steinmetz was a tall, spare man with an Aryan chin and a thick head of ash–blond hair going to silver as he segued from middle to old age. "Mister Fowler," Steinmetz said with precise diction tinged with a German accent. "How may I help you?" He knew, but he insisted on the ritual and being the one to grant favors to a humble civil servant.

"I'd like to speak to Mister Clipp," Fowler said.

"Certainly." Steinmetz's teeth showed in a patronizing grin. "Right this way, please." He parted a curtain that led to the workshop at the back of the store. Beside a tall, imposing safe stood a workbench lit by a single harsh goose–necked lamp.

The safe had Gerhard E. Steinmetz Jewelry stenciled in fancy gilt letters on its door. Why? It obviously wasn't going anywhere else, so who else's could it be?

At the bench, Byron Clipp sat huddled over a deep silver chalice, a scriber in his hand and a binocular headband magnifier over his eyes, his wiry black hair bristling around the straps.

Clipp had the look of a man who spent a lifetime dodging blows to his head. His neck craned forward and his shoulders hunched as he leaned over his work.

The chalice was beautifully made, with graceful curves and a mirror sheen. Its base was wrapped in a chamois to protect its surface, and a wooden screw clamp held it steady as Clipp worked.

On the wall over the bench, Fowler saw a print of Da Vinci's Last Supper, which Clipp was dutifully copying onto the face of the Communion cup.

"Hello, Fowler," Clipp said without looking up.

"How'd you know it was me?"

Without turning his head, he pointed to the chalice. "You cast a recognizable reflection." Clipp set down his scriber, pushed up the magnifier and rubbed his eyes with the heel of his hand.

Fowler peered over Clip's shoulder at the chalice. The work was beautifully detailed. "That's a remarkable job, Byron. A long way from etching the White House."

The corner of Clipp's mouth turned up in a wry smile. "I never did anything as small as a twenty, Fowler. You know my jacket like you know your own resume."

"You never got caught making twenty dollar bills."

Clipp laughed. "That's true too."

"I won't waste your time, Clipp. I have a question."

"Official?"

"Paycheck attached." Fowler lowered his voice. "Why would anyone steal a piece of a twelve–bill plate for twenties instead of the whole thing?"

Clipp's brow creased. "Front and back? One bill? Two?"

"One. Front and back." Fowler counted to four before the engraver said. "Why would anybody steal plates? To make money. If I were you, I'd worry more about where they were going. It's a lot easier to move a three by six segment than a full twelve banger. The plates might be going out of the country."

Fowler chewed his lower lip. "So somebody goes to the trouble to print up a heap of bogus twenties. To make it worthwhile, they have to print a bale of them then smuggle them back into the country. Too little return for too much trouble."

"Wise up, Fowler. You read the papers? There's a war brewing in Europe. Wars cost money. Genuine U.S. plates running twenty-four hours a day? It'd be a lot of work, but you could produce a hundred large in a week. Peddle them on the international currency exchange or launder them through a hundred channels. Buys a lot of bullets."

"You sound like you know a lot more about it than you're telling me, Clipp."

"Nothing more than you could read in the Washington Post."

"You haven't been 'consulting' for somebody else, have you?"

"Who, me?" Clipp raised a bushy eyebrow. "My parole is up in –" He ticked off days in his head. "A hundred and three days. I'm not going back in the joint for anybody's money. Besides," he pointed to the chalice. "I found religion."

"Anything interesting comes up, you know my number."

Clipp grunted. "I'm touched that you trust me."

"As long as I can see both your hands at once."

Fowler nodded to Steinmetz as he left. The jeweler watched as the Inspector crossed the street and got into the Roadster. Then he picked up the phone. "It's Steinmetz," he said. "I need to talk to Tito. It's important."

Tito hung up the phone. So the FBI was on the case already, he thought.

Counting on the rivalry between the two agencies, he had hoped that Treasury would work it on their own, but that was out the window.

Fowler. Tito had heard the name. He was a hotshot investigator and had a rep for cracking the big cases. One more reason to be careful, but he was careful every step. The Plan had to work; Tito's future depended on it. Only one way to make sure. Fowler couldn't interfere if he was dead.

He buzzed Pug on the intercom. "Get Tommy Moon on the phone."

(9)

"So where do we look first?" Kendall said.

"I'd say Stroud's place, since he has some known mob ties."

"Stroud's place it is. We taking my car?"

Fowler nodded. "No room for a prisoner in my loaner, on the off chance we'd nab one."

"And there's no mistaking the Bureau cars for a family on holiday."

The phone on Fowler's desk jangled. "Fowler." His brow creased as he listened. "I see. Thank you." He hung up the phone. "D.C. Metro just fished a floater out of the Potomac. Billy Krajovic."

"That leaves Stroud and Savage."

"Two down and two to go."

The address the BPE had on file for James Stroud was on the outside edge of Georgetown in a neighborhood full of run down tenements on the verge of slum status.

"This is the building," Fowler said. "Apartment 3C,"

The tenement was dirty red brick separated by narrow alleys between two others like it. The stone steps climbing to the double entrance doors were sway-backed with age and wear. Inside, the foyer was dim and shabby. A threadbare carpet covered a cracked tile floor.

"No elevator." Kendall looked around the foyer and noticed a door at the end of a short hallway flanking the stairs. "Back here."

Fowler and Kendall found themselves at a door with a piece of surgical tape across the upper panel. Written in indelible pencil were the words: Milt Kranek Supt.

"Must have flunked out of med school." Fowler rapped on the door with his knuckles. When that got no response, he pounded with his fist, rattling the knob and hinges.

"Yeah, yeah." The voice from inside was a raspy mix of whiskey, cigarettes, and irritation.

The door swung inward to reveal a balding man in baggy trousers, suspenders over his undershirt. A cigarette dangled from the corner of his mouth. Rheumy eyes and a three-day stubble on his receding chin completed the picture. He eyed Kendall and Fowler up and down. "What?" His breath smelled as bad as his armpits.

Kendall flashed his badge. "FBI. I'm Special Inspector Kendall." He jerked a thumb over his shoulder. "This is Inspector Fowler. Do you have a tenant named James Stroud?"

Kranek's eyes narrowed. "Why?"

"Usually we ask the questions, Mister Kranek," Kendall said. "We'd like to have a look at his apartment."

"Got a warrant?"

"I was mistaken," Fowler said. "It wasn't med school; it was law school." Then to Kranek, "The warrant's on the way."

"Wake me up when it gets here." Kranek began to push the door shut.

Kendall caught it with the heel of his hand and shoved it inward, catching Kranek between his shaggy eyebrows. He staggered backward.

"Oh, come in?" Kendall said, loud enough for anyone on the floor to hear. "Why thank you, Mister Kranek. We will." The agents stepped into Kranek's apartment and Fowler shut the door behind them.

Kranek blinked and shook his head to clear it. "You can't just come in here like –"

"Pay attention, Andy Gump, We just did. Now, we don't want to have to break down Stroud's door and make more work for you. The key would be helpful." Kendall held out his hand.

"I know the law."

"Then you know how long a stretch you'd get for impeding a federal investigation."

"Oh, for Christ's sake, Milt, give him the key."

Over Kranek's shoulder, they saw a scrawny woman in a grubby blue chenille bathrobe, her hair in rollers. She cupped a cigarette in the palm of her hand like a con in the exercise yard.

"Stay out of this, Myrtle."

"Shut up and give him the goddamned key."

"Listen to the lady, Milt," Kendall said.

Kranek huffed and dug a ring of keys from his pocket. He flipped them over the ring one at a time til he found the one stamped 3–C. He started to take the key off the ring, but Kendall grabbed the whole works and moved for the door.

"Hey! Give those back!"

"When we're done, Milt. When we're done."

Fowler turned in the doorway and doffed his hat. "Afternoon, Ma'am." He closed the door on the tongue lashing she was giving her husband. "I wouldn't arrest him if I had to. Jail would be a vacation from living with her."

"Agreed." Kendall sighed. "No elevator."

"You said that once already. Travails of the badge. Let's go."

By the time the pair reached the third floor, both were sweating in the airless heat. Behind closed doors, babies cried, radios blared as if to drown each other out, and muffled voices blended with them to make a constant undercurrent of noise. The smell of onions and cooked cabbage permeated the building.

Apartment 3-C was at the end of a hallway lit by a bare bulb whose glass shade was long gone.

Kendall jingled the keys. "Do we knock?"

Fowler gave one cursory rap on the door, counted to ten, shrugged, and said, "Nobody home."

"He ain't there." They turned to see a crone in a faded house dress in the doorway across the hall. "Ain't been around a couple o' days."

Fowler flashed his badge. "Please go back inside, Ma'am."

The old woman hesitated, afraid she might miss something. When she saw the agents draw their pistols, she scuttled back inside her apartment and slammed the door. Kendall and Fowler stood on either side of the doorway, guns at the ready. Fowler held up three fingers. Kendall nodded, hand on the doorknob. Fowler mouthed, "One, two –"

On three, Kendall pushed the door open and the agents sprang into the room, sweeping their pistols left and right.

Nothing.

The apartment smelled of heat and dust and old coffee.

The air was stale and close, windows were closed and blinds drawn. The front room was the biggest, and beyond it a small kitchen opened onto a bathroom with a shower stall and toilet.

A single bed stood under the living room window. It was neatly made, sheet and bedspread pulled up to the pillow. A large wardrobe stood by the kitchen door and in the corner, a green upholstered chair with shiny arms stood beside a small table with a cathedral radio, completing the furnishings.

Kendall snapped on the light switch and the bare bulb in the ceiling fixture cast a harsh light on the room.

Fowler raised the blind and through the fly-specked window caught a bird's eye view of the alley below.

"I'll take the kitchen," Kendall said.

Fowler raised one end of the mattress and then the other, finding nothing there or inside the pillow case. A quick look under the bed showed nothing but dust balls and a pair of expensive but worn out leather slippers. A lush life gone to seed.

Kendall came out of the kitchen with a bag of Eight O'clock Coffee. "Check this out." He spread the bag open and Fowler saw the half buried butt of a palm-sized automatic. Fowler poked into the bag with his fountain pen and hooked the pistol through the trigger guard. He pulled it out and held it to the light. "Must have cost at least three bucks."

"The shells probably cost more than the gun," Kendall said with a snort.

"Lots of them around." Fowler squinted at the chrome plating. "That's funny, or maybe it isn't. It's been wiped."

"Maybe we'll be lucky and he forgot to wipe the cartridges when he loaded it."

Fowler held the little pistol to his nose and sniffed.

"Well?"

"Smells like coffee. It hasn't been fired."

"Just as well. Probably would've blown up in his fist. They're notorious for that."

Fowler dropped the automatic back into the bag. "Let's just say he hasn't shot anybody with it in the last month. Keep looking."

Fowler opened the double door to the wardrobe. To the left were clothes on hangers; two sets of janitor greens and a pair of suits. Three dress shirts hung to the right. Wingtip shoes shared the floor with a pair of overshoes and steel toed brogans. The pedestrian clothes in the closet echoed the theme of the slippers. All were expensive; all were once stylish, and now were worn and shabby from wear, testimony to their owner's former status. Art had described Stroud as a sharp dresser. "He must keep his good clothes elsewhere," Fowler said under his breath.

The drawers were more interesting. In one, under socks and boxer shorts, Fowler found a stack of pin up photos, women in various states of undress. Some were autographed and one had a lipstick kiss on its glossy surface. Near the bottom of the pile was a nude of a pretty blonde. The name Betty Mace was printed in the bottom left corner. It was dedicated to "Jimmy Boy" and signed, "Love, Betty XO."

In the next drawer he found a red cigarette tin. Turkish Elites. It rattled when he picked it up. In it were two pairs of cheap cufflinks, a tie clip, and a half empty matchbook with the words Blue Bunny in silver across the slick cover.

Kendall came out of the kitchen. "Not much else in there. I'd say it's been a week since anybody's been in the place."

"I found this." Fowler held up the matchbook. "Ring any chimes?"

"Sure. It's one of Tito Marcoletto's strip clubs."

" And I'll bet she –" he held up Betty's photo "—works there."

"Maybe they all do. There's a lead worth following."

"I thought you'd say that."

They were about to leave when Fowler hesitated. "Remember when we worked the Tremont case? Where we found the combination to the safe?"

"Yeah."

Fowler rolled back a corner of the rug. Nothing. He rolled back another corner. The same. "Okay, push up on the corner of the wardrobe so I can peel back this corner. Kendall put his shoulder against the heavy wardrobe and tilted it sideways.

"Bingo!"

A strip of adhesive tape held a key to the backing of the rug.

"Now," said Kendall, "all we need to do is find the lock."

Fowler held the key, the matchbook and the cheesecake photos in his hands. "I'm betting these are all on the tail of the same kite."

"I'm betting you're right."

"One way to find out."

(10)

Betty Mace rolled away from Stroud to reach for her cigarettes. The bed springs groaned like a dying man. "How long do you have to stay in this dump?"

"A few more days. You can stay with me if you want to, sugar."

"I'd love to, Jimmy," she said around her cigarette, "but I have to get back to the club tonight. A girl has to work, you know?"

"Yeah, I get it," Stroud grumbled. "You can't wait to take off your clothes for a bunch of sweaty, drooling drunks."

"But they just look not touch, baby. They don't get this." She put her cigarette in the ashtray and leaned over to kiss Stroud on the mouth, then the chin, then the throat. She worked her way on down from there.

In the next room, Pouch shuffled his cards. He would have watched through the keyhole, but he'd seen it all twice already. His incisions ached, but he knew better than to drink the half bottle of whiskey on the table beside him. Get drunk, fall down, rip out the stitches, and you have to start all over again.

The payload was bigger than usual; so was the incision, but so was the pay day. He was knocked out, so he didn't see what the doc sewed up inside him. He had to be careful how he moved because the payload had corners. Whatever it was, it must be pretty valuable because Marcoletto's men took extra special care of him.

From the bedroom, he heard Betty moaning, and wondered if she were faking it. Then the moaning stopped, and Pouch dealt another hand of solitaire.

Betty looked in the mirror over the dresser in Stroud's bedroom. She frowned. Jimmy always messed her makeup.

"Don't worry, honey," Stroud said. "You always look great."

She looked at his pocket watch lying beside his wallet. No time to fool around. She patted her hair a few times, ran a lipstick around her pout and buttoned her blouse. "Gotta go, baby," she said. "Showtime is showtime." She leaned over him for a quick kiss and he grabbed a handful of her hair and pulled her in for a long passionate one. Betty pushed him back on the bed. "Gotta go."

She grabbed her purse and left the bedroom, closing the door behind her. Betty walked through the hearth room of the cabin, a large open area with a wide roughstone fireplace at either end flanked by the bedroom doorways. She was going out the front door when she almost collided head on with a man coming the other direction.

Betty gasped, startled. The man was about Jimmy's height, but something about him seemed all wrong. He was wearing a blood–stained skivvy shirt under suspenders, and his whole person reminded her of a balloon that somebody let half the air out of, or maybe a melting candle. His cheekbones were prominent, but the lower half of his face seemed to droop and sag, reminding her of the wasted dugs of strippers past their prime. He didn't look that old, but the effect gave him jowls like a hound dog and one big wattle under his chin.

"Excuse me, miss," he said, and stepped out of her way, obvious pain in his movements. He held the screen door open for her, and as she passed him, she noticed the flaccid flesh pushing the undershirt between his suspenders and spilling over the waist of his trousers. She felt his eyes on her ass as she walked to the car, trying not to roll her hips. She took her clothes off seven nights a week for an audience, but this guy's ogling gave her the creeps.

Betty looked in the rear view mirror as she pulled away from the hide-out. The misshapen man was still standing in the doorway watching her drive away. So that's the Pouch, she thought as she drove down the rutted lane to the highway. Jimmy had bragged about "the Plan" one night when he'd had a few drinks too many and how it was going to make him rich enough for the two of them to go away together and live in style. But if he had to spend days and nights with a freak like that, it might not be worth it.

From mud to gravel to pavement. Betty pointed her little blue roadster East and didn't look back.

(11)

Savage's apartment was a little more upscale. The building had an elevator. It was old and rickety, but it took Fowler and Kendall to the fourth floor with no problem. This time, the building super came along. Like the building, he was an improvement. His name was Caldwell, and he was eager to help.

"So, Savage is in on something big, huh?" The stout little man said as he ran the elevator.

"Did you say that?" Fowler asked Kendall.

"Nope. Did you?"

"Not that I recall."

"I mean, jeez," Caldwell blurted, "the FBI."

Fowler fixed a hard stare on the super. "We'd rather the whole building not know we're here, Mister Caldwell." He raised an eyebrow. "Get my gist?"

Caldwell's face flushed to the crown of his bald head. "Oh, uh, right. I'll be quiet." And he was, all the way to the fourth floor and down the hall. He stopped at a door halfway to the end and pulled out a master key.

"Hold it," Fowler said. "Protocol." He stood to one side of the door, and Kendall moved to the other. He grabbed Caldwell and yanked him to the side.

"Hey, what's the idea?"

"People get shot through closed doors," Kendall hissed. "Be quiet."

Fowler knocked, gave it a three count, then knocked a second time. "Nobody home." He nodded to Caldwell. "Go ahead."

Caldwell unlocked the door and as it swung inward, started into the apartment. Kendall grabbed him by the collar and dragged him backward. He put a finger in Caldwell's face and said, "Stay," as if he were talking to his pet Airedale.

The agents drew their pistols and on three burst into the room, hammers cocked. Their eyes swept the room. No one.

Caldwell started through the doorway again and Fowler put a hand on his chest and pushed him back into the hallway. "No kibitzers, pal. This is a potential crime scene. Can't have you contaminating evidence." He closed the door in the sputtering super's face and threw the bolt.

Savage's apartment was a little bigger than Stroud's and a little nicer. Instead of a window shade, the window had drapes; faded, but drapes nonetheless. The living room featured an armchair with a reading lamp, a sofa, and a coffee table with a few newspapers and magazines scattered across it along with a stamped tin ashtray in the shape of a five-pointed star.

Fowler picked a cigarette butt from the ashtray and turned it over in his fingers. "Three rings and a crown; Turkish Elite, like the one in the ashtray at the BEP Annex."

"Looks like a clue."

"Here's hoping."

"I'll take the kitchen."

The pair split up. In the closet, Fowler found the same work greens as Stroud's plus a half dozen well made suits, a few with moth holes, and of all things a tuxedo. "How the mighty have fallen," Fowler said under his breath. The shirts and neckties were equally high quality but worn. Rifling the pockets, he found nothing of interest. A broad brimmed fedora and a snap brimmed newsboy hat sat on a shelf above the clothes pole. The cap yielded nothing. Fowler picked up the fedora and turned it over. Running a finger around the inside of the sweatband he found nothing.

Then he removed the lining and found five ten dollar bills. Fowler unfolded them and fanned them out. The bills were old but all five had the same serial number. There's a link, he thought. Counterfeiting? He'd have to run the numbers. If they weren't bogus, they may be loot from a robbery.

Savage's dresser was so neatly organized that it seemed a shame to disturb the drawers. His clothing down to the socks and boxers was better quality and less shabby than Stroud's. It figured. Savage was older and had more time to

Fowler removed the lining and found five ten dollar bills.

accumulate a wardrobe than his younger cohort.

Kendall came in from the kitchen wiping his hands, spots of flower dotting his trouser leg.

"He's been here in the last twenty–four hours. Or someone has."

"Oh yeah?"

"Coffee grounds are still damp in the percolator; no mold yet."

"So Savage woke up, got out of bed, got dressed, drank his coffee, went to work, and robbed the Bureau of Printing and Engraving. It always amazes me that crooks can just go with their every day routine like everything's normal."

"It helps to be a sociopath," Kendall quipped. "So where haven't we looked?"

"Help me move the bed. I want to check under the mattress."

Nothing under the mattress, nothing in the pillow case. Nothing under the rug either.

Kendall went into the bathroom and a minute later came out with a cigar box. "Look what I found on the shelf."

He swung the lid open and inside was a bundle of letters tied with a length of cord.

"Billet-doux? Love letters?"

"Looks it. Kendall untied the string and flipped through the stack of envelopes. "Maybe a lost love. According to the postmarks the most recent one's from two years ago."

"But he kept them all, so whoever she is –"

"Mary Ellen Kemble."

"Mary Ellen Kemble must still figure in Savage's life."

"A slim lead, but a lead."

"Where's Mary Ellen live?"

Kendall peered at a postmark. "Ames, Iowa."

"We'll get the Des Moines office to pay her a visit. Who knows? He might show up there looking for a hideout."

"Doubtful. If I were Savage, I'd be going out of the country, not deeper into it."

"What's that?" Fowler pointed to a scrap of paper in the bottom of the box.

Kendall unfolded it. "Phone number. I feel better already."

"We'll give it a ring from the pay phone in the lobby."

"We still have Krajovic's place to toss. Maybe we'll find more bones to gnaw on there."

Downstairs, Kendall dropped a nickel in the pay phone and dialed the number he found in Savage's apartment. Fowler listened in. The number rang six, seven, eight times. Someone answered.

"Hello?"

"It's Savage," Kendall said. "Any messages?"

"Mister, I don't know any Savage. This is a phone booth on 28th Northwest. I was just walking past when I heard it ring." Traffic noises filled the background. Kendall hung up. "What do you think?"

"A safe phone for contact. We can put a watch on the booth and see who uses it, but I have a feeling it's already served its purpose and Savage won't call it again."

"You're probably right. So what now?"

"Time to visit Krajovic's digs. Maybe dead men do tell tales."

(12)

Tommy Moon sat sweating behind the wheel of his blue Ford sedan. The fake mustache itched like hell in the heat, and threatened to come loose any minute. This was the worst part of the job for Moon, the waiting. He'd spotted Fowler's car, the fancy Cadillac roadster parked down the street from the FBI building.

When Fowler came out, Moon would tail him and watch for his chance. Normally he'd stalk a target for a few days before the hit, but Marcoletto was in a rush.

The late afternoon traffic was slowing as the clock segued into rush hour. Moon was about to move his car to a better spot when he eyeballed his target. The man looked every inch the clean cut FBI type: navy blue suit, striped tie, fedora, and carrying a briefcase under one arm. He looked a little young, but Moon was never good at guessing ages. He reached into his pocket for a silencer and fitted it onto the end of his pistol.

Bobby Lindstrom whistled as he threw his briefcase into the back of the Caddy. His uncle let him drive it for a few days while he was out of town, and Bobby was all too happy for the privilege. The car was a joy to drive. Joan would be impressed when he pulled up in it.

He pulled into the traffic and crept to the next intersection. The light turned green, but no one moved. A delivery van was stalled, blocking the intersection. Over the honking horns, Bobby couldn't hear the approaching footsteps of someone walking alongside the car.

A hand reached over the driver's door, a hand with a gun. A muted bark from the pistol, and Bobby fell forward against the steering wheel, adding his horn to the angry chorus on the boulevard.

(13)

Arthur Savage sat on the bed in Marcoletto's safe house in Glen Burnie, a cigarette dangling from his fingers, his third in half an hour.

On one hand, he was happy to be hidden. Eighteen hours and he'd heard nothing on the radio about the robbery and read nothing in the papers. Marcoletto's men Shimmy and Tuds brought in his cigarettes and a bottle. Savage didn't know why the secrecy, but the cops had to be looking hard for them.

Tuds made Savage nervous. Six-and-a-half feet and one big muscle, Tuds was almost too big to fit through the pipe chase to get him into the Annex. He thought Tuds was going to knock out the Pollak, and almost fainted when the thug drowned Krajovic in the mop bucket. Then the gorilla dragged Krajovic's body out with him. Why?

And then there was Shimmy. Savage thought of him as Tuds' keeper. The slimy little bastard always had that sneer on his face that you wanted to knock off, but you knew if you tried, Tuds would break your arm, your leg, or your neck.

It was tricky, switching the long bolts on the plate over the heating chase for short ones, just enough threads to hold the plate in place but quickly removed. But if anyone checked the plate in the meantime, the bolts were tight and secure.

Unless someone had to take the plate off, nobody would notice, and in the middle of summer with the heat shut down, there was no reason. The result: when it was time, he and Stroud had the plate off in less than a minute. As janitors, they were able to go almost anywhere in the building. They were able to locate all the switches and controls for the alarms, and as the shift chief, Savage had all the keys to the kingdom on a ring on his belt.

One minute he'd be counting his money in his head, and the next he'd think about how crazy the whole scheme was. But who wouldn't be driven crazy by having more money than he could spend one day and nothing the next. Add the irony of working where all of the money was printed and none of it for him; being relegated to the role of glorified garbage man, emptying ashtrays, cleaning toilets.

He'd thought the scheme was a little nuts when Stroud pitched it to him with Tuds standing at his shoulder. He wanted to refuse, but something in Stroud's voice and the look in Tuds' eye told him that if he said no, he'd be dead two minutes later. So he said yes, and now Marcoletto had him stashed in the safe house and promised him a quick ride to Canada with his share of the payoff, a cool twenty–five grand.

There was a click as the key turned in the lock. The door swung open, and Tuds came in with Shimmy, and a little man dressed in a barber's smock and carrying a satchel.

"Time to change your looks," Shimmy said. "This is Antonio, Mister Marcoletto's personal barber." He said something in Italian, and Antonio grinned broadly. "Antonio speaks no English, so whatever you and I say is between us."

Tuds motioned for Savage to get off the bed. He pulled off the sheet and spread it on the floor, then he set a chair in the middle of it. Savage sat in the chair and Antonio buttoned a barber's cape at his collarbone. He hated to part with his full head of wavy hair, but it would grow back.

"When Antonio's done with you, your own ma'll have to look twicet," Tuds said with a chuckle.

Antonio went into the bathroom for a moment and came back with a basin of steaming water. He reached into his satchel and pulled out a shaving mug and brush. Shimmy sat in the easy chair and Tuds slouched against the door jamb.

"Antonio's going to make you temporarily bald," Shimmy said, reaching into his suit pocket. He handed Savage a small packet of papers. "Here's your new I.D.; birth certificate, driver's license, the works. Congratulations. You're now officially Michael McBride."

Savage looked the papers over as Antonio whipped a froth in the mug. "And the money?"

"At the border," Shimmy replied. "Mister Marcoletto wants to be sure you're gone and stay gone."

Savage nodded although he didn't like it. "Fair enough."

Antonio began snipping away at Savage's forelock, the amber hair drifting down the cape and onto the floor. Once the scissor work was done, Antonio stropped his razor and began daubing the foamy soap on Savage's scalp.

Antonio hummed what Savage recognized as an aria from *Pagliaccia* as he scraped away the stubble. A few minutes later, he stood back admiring his work. "*Bene, bene!*" He pulled a hand mirror from his bag and handed it to Savage.

The effect was surprising. Antonio had not only shaved a bald patch in the crown of Savage's head, he had expertly thinned the hair at the edges so that the baldness looked natural. "*Adesso i baffi.*"

"What?"

"The mustache," Shimmy said. "He's gonna shave it off."

Antonio snipped at the mustache, humming as he went. He whipped up the foam and began lathering Savage's whole face.

"I thought he was just going to do the mustache."

"You got stubble," Shimmy said. "A clean mustache would be like a muddy license plate on a clean getaway car."

"I get it."

Antonio scraped away with the razor. In a moment, the shave finished, he looked to Shimmy who nodded approvingly. Then he stepped to the side, and with a deft motion slashed Savage's throat.

Savage tried to cry out, but all he could manage was a choking gurgle as blood sprayed from his neck. He started thrashing and Tuds pinned him to the chair with his catcher's mitt hands. After a frantic thirty seconds, Savage settled down to die.

"We'd've just shot him," Shimmy said, "but the boss wants him hard to recognize when they find him —if they find him."

"And I bet they don't," Antonio replied in perfect English. "That's some of my best work."

(14)

Krajovic's address was a boarding house in the Southwest quarter of D.C. When Fowler and Kendall turned the corner, they saw two D.C. Municipal

Police cars in front of the building.

"Somebody tip off the locals?"

"Beats me," Fowler said. "Let's go find out."

Fowler parked in the next block. He and Kendall badged their way past the uniforms on the stoop. They were halfway up the stairs to the second floor when they saw D.C. homicide detective Ralph Sandrock blocking the top of the stairs. "Plug" Sandrock, as he was known to the D.C. law enforcement community, got his monicker from his build; no neck, no waist, and solid as cast iron.

"Well, well, if it ain't the Rover Boys. What brings you two out of the Ivory Tower?"

"I'm guessing the same person you're here to chase after," Fowler said. "Billy Krajovic?"

"Snappy guess, Fowler."

"I'm a snappy kind of guy."

"That's why we get the big bucks, Plug," Kendall said, "Intuition."

The corner of Sandrock's mouth lifted in a sneer that pushed his skinny mustache askew. "'Says you. So what does the sainted FBI want with a dumb Pollak?"

"Simply pursuing the righteous course of justice," Fowler said, playing dumb, giving nothing away. "I assume you have him up there?"

"Naah, he's downtown."

"Already? He's in custody?"

Sandrock snorted. "He's in the custody of Saint Peter —or Beelzebub. He's on a slab in the City Morgue. Pulled him out of the Potomac this morning chained to a boat anchor. Some angler snagged him, or he'd still be fish food."

Fowler did a three count as if he were digesting the information. "Mind if we take a look upstairs? In the spirit of interdepartmental cooperation, you understand."

"Maybe. Got a warrant?"

"No need. It's already an investigation scene, and we are officers of the law."

"One more time, what do the Feds want with a dead janitor?"

"Not just any janitor, Plug," Kendall said. "A Federal janitor. He's apparently been a bad boy, and now he's a dead bad boy. Gotta figure out why."

"Oh yeah? What'd he do?"

"Can't say right now, but I promise you'll get all the pertinent info."

Sandrock rolled his eyes. "Yeah, right. I know how that shit goes." He let the comment dangle in the air for a few seconds then stepped back, gesturing with both arms like a maitre d' hotel. "Be my guest."

They entered Krajovic's room and saw complete disarray. Drawers were dumped on the floor, the mattress was more off the single bed that on it, and clothes drooped half off the hangers in the doorless closet. Plug slouched in the doorway, arms folded.

"Gotta hand it to you boys," Kendall said, kicking a shoe out of his path, "if not neat, you're at least thorough. Find anything interesting?"

"Not so much as an empty beer bottle. The guy was a Boy Scout for all I can see."

Fowler picked up a letter from the night stand. Before he could read it, Sandrock said, "Letter from Mama Krajovic telling her little boy how much they miss him and thanks for the cash he sent home. Janitor, huh? Must be good bucks pushing a mop."

"How did you identify the body so fast, Plug?"

"He ID'd himself. Tagged his clothes with a laundry marker, first and last name."

Across the room Fowler saw photographs stuck between a cracked mirror and its frame. One was a family portrait; mother, father and six children all dressed for church and looking grimly dignified. The second was a snapshot of a stout but pretty blonde in a bathing suit beside a lake.

The third was the same woman, this time in a dress, sitting on a front porch swing. In this picture, her features were sharp, her cheek bones prominent, and her eyes deep in their sockets. Her dress hung loosely from her shoulders. Fowler pulled it from the frame and turned it over. On the back was written, "Emily, June 3, 1932," and Fowler realized he was looking at a ghost.

He turned to Sandrock. "Not much to see here. Keep us posted, will you, Plug? We'll do the same."

"Maybe next year, huh? I wouldn't hold my breath, Danny boy."

As they returned to the car, Fowler said, "Let's find a phone. I want our team to autopsy Krajovic. Something's not right here."

"I agree. It's too bad the D.C. cops got involved. It'll make it tough to keep a lid on this."

"The Director won't be happy and neither will the D.C. force when we take over the autopsy."

"Perils of the game. No ties in a pissing contest."

"Especially in this town. So, what do you think about Krajovic's death? Murder? Falling out among thieves?"

"Maybe a double cross. The others may have used him as a patsy then killed him to shut him up. That's two janitors counting Metzler."

"We're lucky he turned up so soon," Fowler said. "Otherwise we'd be wasting a lot of time and resources looking for him. Now we can concentrate on Savage and Stroud."

Kendall leaned against the car and lit a cigarette while Fowler stepped into a phone booth down the block to make the call. Another cigarette later, Fowler returned.

"The Director's going to pull rank on the locals and get Krajovic's body to our team to autopsy."

"You were on a long time. What else?"

"You were right. He's furious because Krajovic's death will hit the papers and people are going to start asking questions and connecting dots."

"He should know you can't keep a secret like that forever."

"You'd be surprised."

Kendall stubbed out his cigarette. "As long as I've worked in the Bureau, I guess I shouldn't be."

What Fowler didn't tell his partner was that he made a second call to break his date with Sally.

"Don't tell me," she said when the switchboard put him through." Our date is cancelled."

"Postponed. How about a rain check?"

"If you're lucky." There was a pause then Sally laughed. "No surprise, Dan. The whole building's buzzing and from what little I've heard, you're taking point on something major."

"Can't talk about it on the phone, shweetheart."

"That's the worst Bogart I've heard all day."

"Ma Bell has big ears."

"And a lot of the wrong friends. It's okay, Dan. I'm pulling extra duty tonight too. Tomorrow's another day."

"And tomorrow, and tomorrow, and tomorrow . . ."

"Goes with the badge. Stay alive 'til tomorrow. I want a Blue Flame sirloin smothered in mushrooms."

"Yes, ma'am."

Fowler hung up smiling.

"It's five–thirty, Larry. The Blue Bunny doesn't open 'til eight. I don't know about you, but I'm starved. No time for lunch today."

"Same here. Ready to chase down some supper?"

Dan looked at his watch. "I was going out with Sally tonight, but I can see that's out the window. Let's do it.

"That makes it unanimous."

They found a café called Erma's two blocks away and ordered the Blue Plate Steak Special: steak, fried potatoes, green beans, and apple pie.

"The Director's expanding the net to the whole East coast. I told him about Savage's girl friend in Iowa and he agreed with me to put a watch on Mary Ellen Kemble. He wants Savage and Stroud bad. He –" Fowler stopped in mid–sentence as the waitress came to pour their coffee. "Supper's on the way, gents."

She waddled away, and Kendall said, "I'm guessing he's getting a lot of heat from upstairs. Hitting the BEP threatens public trust in our currency. This comes at a bad time; the economy is still shaky at best, no matter what FDR says at the national hearth. Maybe some foreign power wants to throw a wrench into recovery."

"I just can't see all around this, Larry. If the heist was some international scheme, it would have been less blatant. This caper was as subtle as a train whistle."

"That's a good point. The robbery being overt, we're warned before any foreign entity could have an impact on our economy."

"And why steal the plates for a single bill?"

"We need an expert to examine the tens we found in Savage's hat. Maybe he was a bill poster on the side."

"That would mean an organization. A counterfeiting network takes more than two or three people."

"Marcoletto?"

"Could be. We've got a link between Stroud and one of Tito's strip clubs. For my money, he's where the arrow points right now."

The waitress brought their meals and the agents dug in. Two bites into the meat, Larry said, "I have a suggestion for the menu: rename the Steak Special."

"To what?"

"Steak a la Goodyear. My jaws are getting tired chewing this S.O.B."

"Maybe it's just a tough cow."

"That's a lot of bull."

(15)

The big maroon Buick Club Sedan rolled down a block lined with the monolithic facades of warehouses. A half block ahead, blue light glowed. The sedan passed the building with a huge winking rabbit in blue argon under the flashing words "Blue Bunny." The Buick stopped at the next building, a warehouse with a sign that read "Mainline Wholesale," part of Tito Marcoletto's labyrinth of dummy corporations designed to mask his illicit operations.

A flick of the Buick's headlights, short-long-short, and the warehouse's bay door rolled up. The sedan pulled inside. The door closed, and two men in suits a half size too small for them climbed out. They both carried pump shotguns. The gunmen scanned the interior of the warehouse in all directions and, seeing no peril, backed away from the car.

Tito Marcoletto stepped out. Living up to his reputation for sartorial savvy, Tito cut a striking figure in a perfectly tailored double breasted pinstriped suit. He straightened his flowered necktie for no one in particular and nodded to his bodyguards.

They crossed the warehouse floor, threading through aisles of dust covered crates, most of which were empty props to maintain the pretense of legitimate business. Against the wall shared with the Blue Bunny was a two–story concrete block tower built like a machine gun bunker with a steel door.

The ground floor of the tower was set up like a conference room, but instead of a long table, the room's center was dominated by a green baize poker table. A well–stocked bar occupied one corner, and beside the door, a rack of shotguns, rifles, and a pair of Tommy guns stood at the ready.

"Mix me a highball, Pug," Tito said to one of his men, and started up the stairs to the tower's upper floor. The mobster switched on the light and looked around the room. It was an office that would have graced any corporate executive; plush carpet on the floor, walnut wainscoting and art deco lamps sharing the walls with framed photographs of villages in Sicily.

Marcoletto's polished mahogany desk held only an intercom, a squat black Stromberg telephone, a cut glass ashtray, and a silver humidor. Leather armchairs faced the desk, and Tito's throne-like swivel chair sat behind it.

Red velvet drapes covered windows on two opposing walls. One gave a view of the warehouse floor; the other the show floor of the Blue Bunny. His drink in hand, Tito drew back the drape and looked down into his night club. Below, he saw the staff scurrying around putting the last minute touches on the room before the Bunny opened. The stage was dark, but lights glowed in the orchestra pit where the twelve piece ensemble was tuning and warming up, filling the room with brassy chaos.

Marcoletto sat in his chair, leaned back, and relit his cigar. Pug brought the highball and at a nod from his boss left the office, closing the door behind him. Marcolettto gazed across the room at a photograph of two elderly people in front of a farm house, the hog pen beside it.

I'm a long way from my roots, he thought. My brothers thought I was crazy to come to America, but I showed them all. They're still slaving for some boss for a few lire. But me, I'm the boss, and everybody slaves for me. Who's crazy now?

Loan sharking paid good, and blackmail paid even better, but Tito wanted more. He wanted the respect that came with position, and his scheme would earn him both.

The intercom buzzed. Pug's voice: "Shimmy and Tuds are here."

"Send 'em up."

Tito leaned back in his chair and blew a cloud of blue smoke at the ceiling. The worst part of being the boss, he thought is when other people bungle things and you have to clean it up. The door opened and Tuds came in with Shimmy. Neither took a seat; nobody sat down in Tito's office unless invited.

Marcoletto said nothing. His underlings respectfully waited their turn. Tito eyed them up and down then gave them a barracuda grin. "So, now we're rid of Savage?"

"Yeah. Boss," Tuds answered with a chuckle. "Tony give 'im a real good shave."

Tito's grin went flat. "I hope you didn't throw him in the Pototmac like you did Krajovic," he said through his teeth. "I got word from downtown that the cops fished the Pollack out of the river this morning. I was counting on the Feds wasting time and manpower chasing him a while. The same for Savage."

Tuds's eyes widened. "Gee, Boss, I never …"

Tito held up a hand that cut Tuds off. "That's right. You never. If the heat finds Savage before we're free and clear, you and I are going to have a talk. You understand me?"

Tuds nodded slowly. "Yeah, Boss."

"Now get out of here. Shimmy, you stay."

When Tuds left and closed the door behind him, Tito said, "He's useful, but he's not real bright, is he?"

Shimmy shook his head. "Nope, but he takes orders well."

"So the reason the flatfeet found Krajovic is your orders weren't specific enough. You didn't think either." Tito leaned forward in his chair. "If I have the same problem with Savage I did with Krajovic, I'll have that little talk with you, not Tuds. Got me?"

"Uh, sure, Tito."

"Boss."

"Uh, sure, Boss I got you."

"Go take care of things. Now."

Without another word, Shimmy walked out.

Tito looked down on the Bunny. The doors were open and the crowd was drifting in. Business was always slower this time of the night this time of the year. It was daylight 'til almost nine and many of his customers preferred to slip in after dark. There was lots of cash to be made on the lust of sailors on leave, drunken conventioneers, and wayward husbands, but the Bunny's real rewards came from incognito visits by Senators, Congressmen, and other political bigwigs a thousand miles from their districts and out for a night of illicit fun.

Marcoletto's filing cabinet held a treasure trove of photos of the high and the mighty kissing and fondling the bare bosomed dancers, one Senator even climbing up on stage to dance with his favorite stripper.

Scenes like those don't play well back home in Kankakee, so Tito kept them in reserve. Photos for favors, he called it, and occasionally they paid off big and bought him approval from his bosses.

But Tito wanted more. He wanted to climb the ladder, and short of starting a war, the only way to do that was to curry favor with the people over his bosses, the royalty in Sicily. And if his plan panned out, he would have that favor in spades.

The plan was a masterpiece, but things could always go wrong. The next few days were crucial, and he hoped that Shimmy and Tuds would make sure that Savage wasn't found.

Downstairs, the orchestra fired up and Ralphie, the tuxedoed emcee came out into the spotlight. The chubby bald man bellowed over the microphone, "Gentlemen! And ladies if there are any, it's show time and to lead off tonight's entertainment, give a great big welcome to the delightful, the deluscious, Desiree!"

To claps and whistles and hoots, a tall, leggy blonde swathed in feather boas insinuated her way across the stage to the bump and grind rhythm of the orchestra. Tito pulled the curtain. He'd seen her before. His gaze drifted to the oversized leather sofa where he "auditioned" the strippers. He'd had her before, too. Right now he needed to think.

(16)

Kendall parked the car a block up the street from the Blue Bunny in front of a dingy warehouse. Ahead of them was a dimly lit block surprisingly parked end to end with cars in the loading zones where trucks were parked in the daytime.

"Business is good tonight," Fowler said.

"The Shriners must be in town." Kendall stubbed out his cigarette in the ashtray and climbed out. The stars were out, but the day's heat still radiated from the cracked sidewalks and the soot stained brick facades.

The agents strolled down the street, casual, just a couple of guys out for a night's fun. Ahead in the blue glow of the of the night club's sign they saw a pair of men in suits, their necks too thick to button their collars.

"Tito's boys," Kendall said, a statement, not a question.

"Yeah. I'm sure he's got others up and down the street watching the customers' cars, although a thief would have to be drunk or desperate to work this street. Tito brooks no interference with his clientele."

Two customers approached the bouncers first. The customers walked through the double doors without a word or even apparent acknowledgment from the thugs.

"That's good," Fowler said. "We won't have to badge our way in."

"I got the ultimate badge right here," Kendall said, holding up a ten dollar bill.

When they reached the front door of the Blue Bunny, one of the bouncers gave them a seemingly casual glance as they passed, but Fowler knew that in that glance, he took their measure as a potential problem. Kendall gave him a two-finger salute and the agents opened the door to the sound of a sultry saxophone, the bom-bom-da-bom-bom of the drums and the hoots and whistles of enthusiastic patrons.

"Gentlemen." A wiry little man in a tuxedo stood at a podium to the left of the door. It was well cut, but Fowler could still make out the vague shape of a holster under his left armpit. "Welcome to the Blue Bunny." His oily straight black hair was parted dead center and his dark eyes were deep in their sockets, giving him the look of an evil henchman in a Bela Lugosi movie. His chin looked as if it could split a log.

"My name is Sylvester; they call me Slick. Our cover charge is five dollars."

"I've got it," Fowler said to Kendall, reaching for his money clip. He handed two fives to Slick, who slipped them into a slot in the podium.

"Thank you, sir. Now is there anything else I can do for you? Anything special?" His solicitous emphasis on the last word made him sound like the pimp he was. Over his shoulder they could see a hefty red head rolling her considerable bosom to the visceral beat.

"We were hoping Betty was working tonight," Kendall said, He cupped his hands in front of his chest and raised his eyebrows. "The blond?"

The host gave him a solicitous smile. "You're in luck, gentlemen. Betty Mace will be on a little later. But there's plenty to see in the meantime."

Kendall held out a sawbuck. "Then give us a table with a view."

With a flick of his fingers, Slick made the bill disappear up his sleeve like a magic trick. "Certainly. Right this way, gentlemen."

For a converted warehouse, the Blue Bunny was a pretty nice nightclub. A stage stretched across the far end of a good sized room with a bar along the left side. A runway brought the ladies out among the tables to give the customers a satisfactory look at their goods. The walls were painted navy blue to mask the raw look of the terra cotta blockwork and they featured huge baby blue cartoon rabbits engaged in every sort of misbehavior.

Slick led them around the periphery to avoid blocking anyone's view of the show. As they rounded the room, Fowler got a better look, noting that no exits were visible. He figured that in a fire or a raid, everyone moved through the curtained alcoves at either side of the stage, through the dressing rooms, and into the alley behind. High up the north wall, he noticed a wide window.

Slick seated them at a table near the runway. "Your waitress will be with you right away. Enjoy your evening." He bowed at the waist and disappeared.

Fowler twitched his head. "Up the wall —a private viewport."

"Maybe to entertain special guests," Kendall replied over the raucous music.

"Or just to keep an eye on this joint. I bet if you trace title on the building next door far enough, you'll find the deed in Tito's back pocket."

The redhead concluded her act by turning her back to the audience and doing a straddling bend over that left nothing to the imagination. She winked at the audience between her knees, gathered the pieces of her costume, and scampered offstage, blowing a kiss over her shoulder.

A midget in white overalls and a janitor's cap came out with a push broom to sweep up the coins and bills the customers threw on the runway.

"Now there's a career to envy," Kendall said with a laugh.

A cute young waitress in fishnet stockings, a short ruffled skirt, and nothing else, came to their table with a tray. "Hi, fellas; I'm Cora. Drinks for you?"

"Nothing for me. You, Larry?"

Cora's smile flattened. "Two drink minimum apiece, guys."

Kendall shrugged. "Okay, gin and tonic, twist of lime."

"Same for me."

The smile returned. "Right away. Enjoy the show." She jiggled off and Kendall said, "No warning sign at the door."

"I guess it's geared to chase the riff-raff out."

Kendall looked around at the crowd. "I'm not sure it's working."

The crowd was mixed; working class Joes beside men in business suits beside young bucks in collegiate letterman sweaters. Most of them leering, catcalling, and drunk.

At that moment, an egg–shaped comedian waddled onstage. He was bald except for a fringe of orange like a circus clown and thick glasses perched on his bulbous nose. He wore a black and yellow checkered suit and a flowered necktie as wide as an ironing board. The emcee introduced him as Fat Jack.

The comedian launched into a raft of jokes disparaging his frigid wife while waiting for someone in the crowd to heckle him.

"Two men were sitting at a bar and staring into their drinks. One said, 'Hey, look at that. Have you ever seen an ice cube with a hole in it before?' The other said, 'Yeah. I'm married to one for.'"

"Get off the stage, asshole!" A big man in shirtsleeves bellowed. It was just the opening Fat Jack wanted. "What are you doing here, Jethro? Somebody lock the sheep in the barn?" What followed was fifteen minutes of insult and indignity punctuated with every obscenity and innuendo imaginable as Fat Jack singled out audience members.

"Nice tie!" someone shouted.

"Yours too," Fat Jack snapped. "Couldn't guess your weight either, huh, whistle-dick?"

The drinks arrived. "That'll be ten bucks, guys," Cora said, setting the drinks on the table, making sure her breasts swung side to side as she did. Fowler gave her a ten dollar bill and she frowned. "I'll be back when you're ready for your next round," she said and sashayed to the next table where she was better appreciated.

Kendall chuckled. "She was hoping for a twenty and 'keep the change.'"

"Yeah, but I don't know how I could justify that on my expense account."

The moment Fowler was watching for arrived. Fat Jack made a wisecrack about the similarity of a customer's nose with his manhood: "long as my schlong."

The customer jumped up, knocking over his chair and slamming into the next table, spilling drinks. He started for the runway, but before he got three steps, two men with builds like toll booths caught him by the arms and half-dragged, half-carried him out the back of the room.

"That's what I wanted to know," Fowler said, "where the hired help is located. Nobody came through the curtains, so there doesn't seem to be any muscle backstage. The next time they're busy, that's where we'll go."

"Not 'til we're sure Betty's back there. She may not be working tonight, despite what Dracula said."

"In the meantime, maybe we'll get lucky and Stroud'll show up."

"You don't sound hopeful."

"I'm not."

Ralphie came out and said with a laugh, "That's enough from that horse's ass. Here's a little lady you'll like a whole lot better. Here they are, fellas, Ruby Jean!"

A short blonde swaggered out of the wings swathed in at least a dozen silk shawls that dangled like multicolored fringe from her torso. She strutted up and down the runway, smiling and waving to patrons, calling some by name. They hooted and whistled in reply.

She stood at the end of the runway and the drummer rolled on his snare. The horns played a fanfare and at its crescendo, Ruby Jean pulled the boas aside to reveal breasts that hung to her hips. Silver stars that sparkled in the spotlight were pasted over her aureoles.

Ruby Jean swung one breast in a circle, and punctuated by a rim shot from the drummer, threw it over her shoulder. She followed with the other to the delight of the crowd.

At that moment, Cora returned, making a point of blocking the view of the runway. "Another round, guys?"

"More of the same," Kendall said. "Hey, Cora." He held out a five, when's Betty Mace come on?"

"A little later," she said, smiling again." Cora picked up the empty glasses and hustled off, tucking the tip in the waistband of her skirt.

Ruby Jean did a few more tricks with her assets to the cheers of the crowd. She finished by pulling off the stars and sending them spinning into the crowd then putting both nipples in her mouth.

"Tough act to follow," Kendall said.

"The advantage of being unique."

"See anyone you recognize?"

"No Stroud, but back in the corner, I'd swear the guy with the dark glasses and bad wig is Senator Walsingham."

Kendall craned his neck. "Could be."

The room got smokier, the music got louder, and the crowd got drunker. Two more acts, and the emcee's voice boomed, "And now gents, the lady you've all been waiting to see, the de-lightful, de-lovely, de-lectable, de-luscious, Betty Mace!"

The band struck up a brassy number with lots of slide trombone. The spotlight followed Betty as she emerged from the wings and crossed the stage to the runway. She wore a red sequined evening gown slit to her hip, white lace gloves to her biceps, and a jeweled tiara in her thick mane of blonde hair.

Instead of swaying seductively, Betty strode out with her nose in the air like British royalty, as if the clapping, whistling audience were beneath her attention. Fowler turned in his chair. "I'll watch for Stroud. You watch Betty."

"I was going to suggest the same thing."

Betty spread her arms in a welcoming gesture and gracefully turned a full rotation, her haughty posture telling the sweating, ogling men, "You want all this, but you'll never touch it in a hundred years."

Where the previous women were cheap and tawdry, Betty radiated class, a sultry sophistication that transcended the bawdy nightclub and made the raucous crowd hold its collective breath in anticipation.

The band shifted to a bluesy slow burner that seemed to pulse with pure lust. Betty scanned the upturned faces of the crowd from the bottom of her eyes for a moment then slowly began tugging at the fingers of her left glove one at a time. The glove slowly slid down her arm and came free. Betty twirled it for a moment then dropped it on the runway. No gifts for her devotees.

Ruby Jean pulled the boas aside...

No sign of Stroud. Fowler turned back toward Betty in time to see her tug off her right glove an inch at a time with her teeth. The formerly rowdy crowd seemed transfixed by the sight.

"She puts on a good show," Fowler said.

"Her photo doesn't do her justice."

A shrug of her shoulders, and Betty's gown slid down her body to her feet, leaving her clad in black stockings and a black lace teddy. She stepped free of the gown revealing black patent leather shoes with baby doll heels.

Her hands slid down her sides and hips and her thighs as she crouched forward, deepening her cleavage. Her smoldering eyes swept the room, challenging, mocking the spellbound crowd. Then as the music intensified, with agonizing slowness, she began unbuttoning the front of her teddy.

"Take it off!" a man shouted, and Betty waggled an admonitory finger at him. She began rebuttoning the teddy to howls of dismay from her fans. Betty shrugged and crossed her arms, tapping her toe.

The patrons made it rain. Silver dollars bounced and rolled on the runway, and crumpled bills flew through the air. Betty stood unmoving until the last silver dollar rolled down the runway and fell flat at her feet like a sacrificial offering. She nodded her head and the music resumed. She began again to undo the buttons.

When the teddy was unbuttoned to the waist, the music stopped and the drummer began a roll. Betty took the shoulder straps of the lacy garment between her thumbs and forefingers. With a cymbal crash, she pulled the straps aside and the teddy drifted to the floor leaving Betty clad in only a sequined G-string and heels. The patrons howled.

The music began again, this time a primal rhythm with horns that wailed from Mankind's savage past. Betty Mace writhed and slithered as if the air around her were a gelid mass, her scarlet lips parted, as her tongue rolled sensuously around them.

Her thumbs hooked in the G-string as she cocked one hip then the other, The crowd was screaming now. Her eyebrows raised. Silver dollars clinked on the runway.

She nodded and ever so slowly began inching the G-string lower. Then in an instant, she pulled it down and the next instant, the spotlight went out, and the runway went dark. The band shifted gears to a lively exit tune, and the emcee boomed, "Let's hear it for the Burlesque Queen of D.C., boys, Betty Mace! She'll be back again later, with even more!" The applause was wild.

"That's good news," Fowler said. She's not leaving the theater for a while. All we have to do is wait."

"For what?"

"A distraction. As drunk and horny as this crowd is, we won't be waiting long."

The waitresses were circling the tables, making a point of rubbing against the customers. Fowler figured serving drinks was only half of their job.

Fat Jack returned, showering insult and abuse, and he was followed by a sinuous Oriental woman who did tricks on a leather armchair that would astound a gymnast.

A burly, red–haired sailor stood up near the back and yelled, "I'm in love." He lurched toward the runway, and the bouncers converged on him. The sailor turned out to be a little more than they expected. He yanked his arm from the grip of one and decked the other with a roundhouse that sounded like a sledgehammer driving a tent stake. The second bouncer sapped him from behind and sent the sailor staggering into a table, spilling drinks and knocking patrons off their chairs.

Before the bouncer could hit him again, the sailor's four shipmates ran to his rescue. The bartenders leapt over the bar and from the entrance, the street thugs came running. According to the rules of musicianship, the band kept playing and played louder. The stripper followed their lead and continued distracting the crowd with her gyrations.

Chairs were swung and bottles broken as the fight spread. Half the customers jumped up and retreated to the sides of the room. The other half joined in the brawl.

"Let's go."

Fowler and Kendall slipped along the wall toward the alcove at the right of the stage. Two men in overalls, stage hands, burst through the curtains carrying Louisville sluggers and passed them in the opposite direction.

"There's two more we don't have to worry about," Kendall said.

"They'll be busy long enough." He and Kendall ducked through the curtains. Down a short, dark hallway, they found the dressing rooms. The hallway opened into a common area with lighted mirrors and costume racks. Some of the women were touching up their makeup and fixing their hair. Others were standing around smoking cigarettes and talking in small groups. Most were in costume ready to go onstage, but a few wore bright robes they didn't bother to fasten. The smell of cheap perfume hung in the air and made Fowler's nostrils twitch.

The music drowned out the sound of the fight out front. The strippers looked up at Fowler and Kendall then went back to their conversations and makeup. Apparently they were used to backstage visitors. Fowler scanned the women, and not seeing Betty Mace, looked to the dressing room doors. The third one had the name Betty written on it in crimson lipstick beside a gold star he recognized as a pasty.

He and Kendall barged in, startling Betty, who was lounging in a chair. The sweetish scent of marijuana filled the room. "Who the hell are you?" She jumped up, clutching the front of her robe. "Who let you back here?"

Larry grinned. "Uncle Sam." He flipped open his badge folder. "FBI. Special

Agent Kendall. This gentleman is Special Agent Fowler."

"We won't take up too much of your time, Miss Krasicki."

At the use of her real name, Betty flinched.

"We just want to ask you a few questions."

"About what?"

"Your pal James Stroud."

"Never heard of him."

Kendall plucked a photograph from the makeup mirror. It was a black and white in a cheap cardboard frame with the words CLUB LA-JA in gilt letters. It showed Betty cuddled up to a smiling Stroud, raising glasses in a toast to the camera.

"Wanna revise that statement?"

"I —I –" she stammered.

"When was the last time you saw your boyfriend?"

"He's not my –"

Her answer was cut off by the entrance of a hulking thug in a black turtle-necked sweater who came through the door holding a baseball bat. The ridges of scar over his piggy eyes tagged him as an ex pug. "You ain't allowed back here," he rasped. "These mugs botherin' you, Miss Betty?"

"Yeah, Tooney. Get 'em out of here."

Tooney held the bat across his chest and started to shove Fowler toward the door. "You heard he lady. Out, Mac." He turned his eyes toward Kendall. "You too, bud."

Fowler caught the bat by its ends, one hand up and one hand down, using Tooney's grip to spin the heavy end to connect with the side of the bouncer's jaw.

Tooney staggered backward, crashing into the makeup table and scattering tubes and vials. He rebounded, throwing a left hook at Fowler, who slipped the punch and stepped in to land a solid right to Tooney's chin. Betty's champion landed flat on the floor. Giving him his due, Tooney was tenacious. He rolled to a crouch and rushed Fowler, driving his shoulder into the agent's mid section.

The two bounced off the wall and landed on the linoleum, gouging and punching. Tooney pushed the agent off him and his hand dove into his pocket and came out with brass knuckles. He swung a roundhouse at Fowler's's head, but missed his target. Betty stared in horror, and Kendall leaned against the wall, arms crossed.

Fowler stomped Tooney's ankle and the bouncer roared in pain. He stag-gered a little and Fowler pressed the advantage. He threw a forearm under Tooney's chin as he hooked his leg behind his knees. In a second. The thug was on his back with the agent's knee in his diaphragm. Tooney tried to tag Fowler with the knuckles, but Dan kept his face out of reach. Failing that, Tooney quit swinging and struggled to get Fowler off him so he could breathe. Two hard lefts to the jaw and Tooney's eyes rolled back in his head.

The noise of the fight had drawn attention. One of the girls looked in, saw the situation, and ran screaming for help. "Time to go," Fowler said as he stood, brushing himself off. Then to Betty, "We'll be in touch, Miss Krasicki. Don't leave town."

They stepped over Tooney and found the exit at the end of the dressing rooms as the sound of running feet came down the corridor.

As they walked out of the alley behind the Blue Bunny, Kendall said, "That was productive."

"Why didn't you sap that gorilla before he messed up my hair?"

"You were doing fine, Dan. Why spoil the fun? We'll haul Betty in later. Right now, we have some work to do before the second show." He held up the key they'd found in Stroud's apartment. "Bet me it doesn't unlock her apartment door?"

"Not on your life."

(17)

Upstairs, Tito was livid. Betty cowered in a chair in front of Tito's desk as he paced behind it. "FBI?" he shouted. "FBI?" He turned to Slick. "How the hell did they get in here?"

Slick knew better than to shrug. "They were paying customers, Boss. The clientele we get sometimes, we don't ask for I.D."

He fixed his glare on Betty, who cringed. "What did they want?"

"They asked me about Jimmy, had I seen him."

Tito ground his teeth. Things were going south in a hurry. How did the Feds connect him to the heist so fast? It had to be the dame.

"Before I said anything, Tooney came in to throw them out, and one of them decked him."

"How did they know about you and Stroud?"

"I don't know," Betty blurted. "I –"

"Did they give you their names?"

"The one who knocked Tooney out said his name was Fowler. The other guy was Kendall."

Tito's jaw clenched. Fowler? The sound of the name was like pouring scalding water on him. Tommy Moon phoned in the word that Fowler was dead. What the hell was going on? He jabbed a finger at Slick. "You, watch the door better." Then to Betty, "You, get out of Stroud's life and stay out. No calls, no visits, no love notes, nothing. Get me?"

"What'll I tell him?"

"You ain't listening to me. You don't tell him jack! I'll tell him."

"But I love him, and he loves me."

"This ain't Backstage Wife, honey. You got another show to do. Get downstairs while your nose still aims forward."

Betty stood, trembling. "I—I—"

"Get out!"

Pug ushered Slick and Betty out and closed the door behind them. "What now, Boss?"

"Get that screw-up Moon on the phone, and get me the lowdown on Fowler and Kendall. I have to think a while."

Tito pulled the curtain aside and looked down at the club. Fat Jack was hurling barbs at the crowd, and the waitresses were shaking their titties at the drunks, the fight forgotten. Business as usual.

He smacked his fist into his palm. One more hitch in a good plan. Leave it to a piece of tail to louse things up. Love. Yeah, Stroud loved her all right, right after himself, money, and whatever bimbo caught his eye in the meantime. He'd think about her later. Right now, Fowler was his big concern. Just three more days and Pouch would be on the boat. He couldn't let Fowler mess things up.

Downstairs, on her way to the dressing room, Betty fought back tears. How could she give up Jimmy? And how could he give her up? She had to do something. There was no phone at the safe house; all she could do was go to him, and it had to be now.

Betty Mace's building was on the fringe of the Northwest quarter in a better than average neighborhood. "Stripping must pay pretty well," Kendall quipped.

"Too bad you're male. You could quit the Bureau and live like a queen."

"Naah. No place to hide a gun.

"Priorities."

"I'll go up. You wait and watch."

"I'll signal with the horn if she shows up. Thirty-two Plymouth, right?"

"Yeah. Blue roadster. Watch for it."

The apartment was in a six-story brownstone. No doorman, but there were plants in the lobby that were green, and the carpet was fairly new. Inside the entrance door, a set of brass mailboxes clung to the wall. Fowler ran his finger across the first and second rank before he found "Krasicki —5C."

Fowler rang for the elevator. The car was empty, like the fifth floor hallway. The sounds of music, conversation and everyday life filtered under the doors. 5C overlooked the street below. Fowler put an ear to the door. No sound.

"Here goes nothing," Fowler said, inserting the key.

It fit.

Fowler switched on the lights. Betty's apartment was tidy and for all the world looked like it might belong to a librarian or a choir director. The place was spotless and furnished in middle–class good taste. "Definitely a woman's touch," Fowler said under his breath.

The furniture included a matching blue chenille sofa and armchair sharing a coffee table with neat ranks of magazines, movie mags and scandal rags. A console radio stood against the wall between a telephone stand and a coat tree with a few hats.

On the radio cabinet, Fowler saw a framed photo of what had to be Betty's parents. Their faces had that forced dignity you found in Midwestern people too far from either coast to be infected by jaded urban sophistication. Fowler imagined the Krascickis seated on either side of their radio in the parlor only for the farm report, the weather, FDR's Fireside Chats, and Father Coughlin. They would no doubt be horrified at what their daughter did to afford her apartment.

Like the living room, the bedroom was neat. The brass railed bed was covered with a purple satin duvet and piled with ornamental pillows. A dressing table with a lighted mirror like the one she used at the Blue Bunny stood in one corner. Its surface was cluttered with makeup and bottles of nail polish. Tucked into the mirror's frame was a snapshot of Stroud lounging against the fender of a touring car, a cigarette dangling from the corner of his mouth, the very image of insouciance.

A calendar with a color picture of Paris hung beside the mirror. The twenty-third was circled in eyebrow pencil. Three days away, Thursday. What did that mean? Under the bed, he found a suitcase packed with essentials and ready to travel at a moment's notice. Something would happen on the twenty-third, but she was ready to leave at any minute in the meantime.

Fowler carefully rifled a drawer full of lingerie, lifting things one pile at a time and setting them back in place. Under a nest of lacy brassieres, Fowler found a small chrome plated .25 automatic with pearl handles. He dropped the clip and emptied it. He pulled back the slide and a live round popped out and landed on the carpet. He replaced the pistol and was going through the next drawer when he heard Kendall's signal; three short blasts on the horn, one long. Again. Time to go.

He turned the key in the lock and looked down the hallway to the elevator. The arrow was swinging clockwise between two and three. He ducked into the stairwell and watched through the glass in the fire door.

The elevator doors opened and Betty hurried to her apartment. She fumbled with her key and finally, the door swung inward. She disappeared inside and slammed the door behind her.

Fowler slipped out of the stairwell and took the elevator to the building's lobby. It was a good bet that Betty was grabbing the suitcase and would be coming out any minute. As he stepped out of the building, he saw Betty's blue roadster parked beside a fire hydrant.

The intercom buzzed. Slick's voice, reedy over the intercom: "Boss, Betty's gone."

"Whattaya mean she's gone?"

"She ain't in the dressing room or backstage. It was time for her show and she wasn't in the wings. Nobody's seen her."

"Send Shimmy and Tuds up here." He snapped off the intercom.

Tito ground his teeth. He used Betty to lure Stroud into the plot, but he should have shut the romance down before it got this far. Things were getting more complicated by the minute.

There was only one place she'd go, and that was to Stroud. He should have never let her go to the hideout to see him. Now she knew the way. Damned broads.

Shimmy and Tuds came in, eyes wary.

"Betty Mace skipped on me. And I figure she's heading for Stroud. Go find her and bring her back here. He handed Shimmy a slip of paper. "Here's her address."

Shimmy studied the paper as if it were a puzzle, Tuds peering over his shoulder.

"Whattaya gawkin' at? Move your asses!"

Two minutes later, the mobsters were in the car heading for the Northwest Quarter.

"Stupid dame," Shimmy muttered.

"Yeah, but she looks good. I'd like some of that myself."

"From the look on the boss's face, she ain't gonna live long. Maybe he'll throw her to us on her way out."

Traffic was heavy, and Shimmy smacked the steering wheel in frustration. Every minute they lost was one more she had to get away, and he was afraid to come back empty-handed. He swore as the light ahead of him turned red.

"Take it easy, Shimmy. We're almost there."

"She see you?" Kendall asked as Fowler climbed into the car.

He shook his head. "Nope. I wish I'd had more time, but we can always come back later. I have a feeling she'll be leaving any minute and won't return." He told Kendall about the calendar and the suitcase. "She left the Bunny without doing her second show. I think we poked a stick in the hornet's nest. I'm betting she's going to Stroud."

"If she does, so much the better."

They pair didn't have to wait long. Within five minutes, Betty came out of the building with her suitcase in one hand and a makeup bag in the other. She threw her luggage behind the seat, climbed into the roadster, and quickly drove away.

"Let's go."

Before Kendall could start the engine, a big sedan pulled up at an angle to the curb, blocking the street. Two men jumped out, one small and the other the size of a phone booth. They looked up and down the street then rushed into the building.

Fowler jotted their license number down. We'll look up those two later. Get after Betty."

Kendall threw the car into reverse and raced to the end of the block, narrowly missing a half dozen parked cars. "She turned right. Head for the next parallel street." They crisscrossed D.C.'s perfect grid of streets for half an hour, but Betty's roadster was nowhere to be seen.

(18)

A half mile away, Betty was making tracks for the fastest way out of town. She wiped a tear from the corner of her eye. She wasn't crying anymore. That son of a bitch Marcoletto, she thought. Who does he think he is, God? Playing with people's lives like he does. She blew her horn, weaving in and out of traffic.

Betty couldn't call Jimmy. There was no phone in that glorified shack, but that meant Marcoletto couldn't call him either. Her only chance was to get to Jimmy first, no matter what it took. And if Tito Marcoletto was going to ruin their plans, she'd make damned sure she'd ruin his.

She patted the pocket of her jacket and felt the little pearl handled automatic Jimmy had given her. Marcoletto's thugs had guns, but so did she.

Betty's taillights had just disappeared around the corner when Shimmy wheeled the big Plymouth sedan to the curb at an angle. He and Tuds jumped out and left the car blocking the street. The pair rushed into Betty's building. "Take the stairs," Shimmy said, "in case she tries to get out that way. I'll take the lift." Tuds ducked into the stairwell as Shimmy stepped into the cage.

The fifth floor hallway was empty. Shimmy strode down the hall, eyeing the brass number plates on the apartment doors. There it was, 5C. He rapped softly on Betty's door. No response. He knocked again, harder.

Tuds came out of the stairwell, red-faced and panting. "She in there?"

"Dunno. Nobody answered."

Tuds hammered the door with his fist. "Hey! Open up!"

A man in a white dress shirt and suspenders, newspaper in his hand, came from the apartment across the hall. "What's going on here? What are you fellows doing?"

Tuds spun on his heel and caught the man square in the mouth with his fist. The tenant sat on the floor, dazed, still holding the newspaper, blood dripping on the sports page.

A woman screamed, "Albert!" and ran to him sobbing. Another woman said, "I'm calling the police." She ran into her apartment and slammed the door, Shimmy heard the snick of the deadbolt.

Tuds glared at the other tenants who had come out, and they retreated down the hall. Shimmy grabbed his arm. "C'mon. Let's get outa here."

They didn't wait for the elevator. Tuds and Shimmy clambered down the fire stairs and ran out the front door of the building. They jumped into their car and in seconds they were gone.

"Now what?" Tuds said. "Back to the Bunny?"

Shimmy shook his head. "Uh-uh. We ain't goin' back to the Boss empty handed. Betty's goin' to Stroud. We know where Stroud is. Odds are good we'll find her there."

Fowler and Kendall realized that Betty was out of sight and out of reach.

"We'll have to put out an APB on her car.," Kendall said.

"Find a phone. We really need to get the Bureau to put two-ways in our cars."

"Agreed. Why don't we go back to Betty's apartment. We can phone from there."

"Good idea."

Kendall wound through the evening traffic and in a few minutes pulled to the curb in front of Betty's building. The street was quiet and deserted, but upstairs, the fifth floor hallway was a different story. Tenants milled around buzzing with agitated conversation. A man sat propped against the wall, a bloody towel pressed against his face. Beside him, a weeping woman sat with an arm around his shoulders.

Fowler flashed his badge and the crowd got quiet. "What happened here?"

Several people started talking at once. Fowler raised a hand. "One at a time, please."

A tiny-grey haired matron in a housecoat said, "I'm Agnes Smith. I live in 5D.These two men, a big one and a little one, started pounding on Miss Krasicki's door and shouting. Well, the big one did anyway for her to open up. It was so loud I thought they were at my door.

"I looked out the peephole and didn't see anybody, so I opened the door a crack and saw the men at Miss Krasicki's apartment. About then, people were coming out into the hall, and Albert —Mister Kensington —asked them what they were doing, and the big one hit him. I ran inside and bolted the door."

Kendall crouched beside Albert, who was awake but dazed. "Let me see it."

Albert took the towel away.. His teeth and gums showed through a lip split to his nose. His wife saw the damage and began to sob all over again.

"Has anyone seen the tenant from 5C?"Fowler asked.

A woman nodded. "Yes. She stopped in for a few minutes around five o'clock and left again."

"And did she come back after that?"

A rangy man in a conductor's uniform said, "Yeah. I just come home from my shift a little bit ago. The Missus gimme the trash to take to the chute, and I saw Betty come outta her place with a couple suitcases. She got on the lift."

The elevator bell chimed, and two D.C. uniforms stepped out.

Fowler identified himself and Kendall. "We came here on another matter. It's all yours." Then to the tenants, "These officers will take your statements."

On the way to the lobby, Kendall said, "Too bad we didn't get in for a second look."

"I didn't want to explain why I had a key to the place, or why we're here in the first place. We'll come back later when things quiet down. Now, let's find a phone." Fowler rifled his pockets. "Got a nickel, Larry?"

"Roll of 'em in the glove box. Just like the Boy Scout motto: be prepared." Kendall chuckled. "Nice to wrap your fist around, too."

They found an all–night diner two blocks over and went in. "Get us a couple of coffees while I call home." Kendall nodded and ambled to the counter while Fowler found the phone booth.

He was back in five minutes. "The Bureau's putting out an APB on Betty Mace's car. If she's on the road, the Staties'll find her."

"And if she isn't?"

"We'll find her."

"I hope we so, before Marcoletto's people do. I have a hunch she's got a good reason to run."

The soda jerk brought the coffees. Kendall laid a buck on the counter. "That cherry pie looks good. Bring me a slice."

"Me too," Fowler said. "If Betty's been shacking up with Stroud, she may know what he's up to and how it's connected to Marcoletto and company."

"Possible." Kendall sipped his coffee and grimaced. "And I thought the office coffee was bad. This stuff could grow hair on your fingernails. I hope the pie is better."

"It may be tough to get Betty to turn on Stroud, but if she thinks Marcoletto's a threat, maybe she'll turn on him."

"That could work in our favor. In the meantime, we need to toss Betty's place down to the last toothpick."

The kid brought the pie. Looks were deceiving.

"Finish your pie and we'll go back there. Things should be quiet by now."

Kendall put a dime on the counter. "Oh don't be a miser, Larry. The coffee isn't his fault."

"You're right." He laid another dime beside the first. "Let's roll."

The hallway outside Betty Mace's apartment was empty when Fowler and Kendall got off the elevator. Fowler unlocked the door and the two were inside before anyone knew they were there.

"Which room first?"

"This one, I guess," Fowler said. "Just don't make too much noise. I don't want the neighbors calling the D.C. boys back."

The agents began methodically turning the living room upside down, lifting every rug, removing every sofa cushion, and dumping out every vase and ashtray. "Not much here," Kendall said.

"Nope. let's try elsewhere."

In the kitchen they opened every drawer and cabinet and dumped every canister on the counter; coffee, flour, sugar, tea —nothing. "I'm starting to think we aren't going to find much here, if anything," Fowler said, sweeping a mound of cornflakes back into the box. "We still have two rooms to go. Let's do it and get out of here."

The bathroom yielded nothing but a rubber bladder Kendall speculated was a birth control device and a bottle of aspirin. "Looks like nothing here," he said, replacing the lid on the toilet tank.

"Let's try the bedroom."

In the back of her nightstand drawer, Fowler found two things of interest, a stack of letters bound with a white ribbon, and a small address book bound in red leather.

"Shouldn't that be black?" Kendall said, looking over Fowler's shoulder as the agent thumbed through the pages.

Fowler didn't laugh. "Look at these names. There are Senators, Congressmen, business moguls, foreign ambassadors."

"And Stroud, I bet."

Fowler turned a few more pages and in the S section they found the address for Stroud's apartment. "There he is."

"Better take that with us, Dan. I'd bet a week's vacation the Director will want to see hat personally."

"I'd say book your hotel in Havana."

They left as quietly as they arrived and were unnoticed by the building tenants. Back in the car, Fowler said, "So much for clues and evidence. Maybe we'll catch a break and the Staties'll spot Betty's car on some lonely road or parked at a motel."

"That'd speed things up. Time to call in one more time then call it a night. I don't want to go back to the office. We might end up there til morning."

Fowler chuckled. "Larry, where's your sense of responsibility?"

"It went off duty at eleven o'clock. There's a booth. Make your call."

The call to the Bureau was uneventful.

"Well?"

Fowler shook his head. "No news on Betty, Savage, or Stroud. There was a message for me from Cooper. He said to call him in the morning, so nothing's shaking there. And there was a message for you from someone named Carole. She wants you to call back no matter what the hour."

"Carole, huh?" Kendall grinned. "Maybe tonight won't be a total loss.

"It's been a long day. I'm going to bed."

Kendall grinned again. "Me too."

(19)

Betty looked at the fuel gauge. Still a quarter tank. Enough to get to Jimmy and if her luck held, she'd get to the hideout before Marcoletto's men did. The two lane blacktop road was so far out in the sticks that there wasn't even a center line painted on it. Trees lined both sides, with an occasional house or farm to break the monotony. She didn't have any idea what to do once she got to Jimmy, but he'd know and they'd do it. That scar-faced prick Marcoletto —he thinks he owns us all, she thought. I'll show him.

The deer came out of nowhere. It ran into the middle of the road and froze. She screamed and stomped the brake pedal, but she wasn't quick enough. The tires squealed and the roadster hit the deer full on, throwing it onto the hood. The car skidded to a stop and the deer stared Betty in the eye through the windshield. It twitched a few times and then lay still.

Betty climbed out of the car and stepped back. The front of the roadster was smashed, the radiator torn loose from the impact and steam gushing from the engine. The left front fender was crumpled, pushed into the tire, which had sunk to the rim.

"Oh God!" Betty sobbed. "Jimmy! Jimmy!"

Headlights. There was still some hope. Maybe whoever it was could help her get the car back on the road, or maybe give her a ride, or maybe —she patted the pistol in her pocket —just hand over his keys.

The approaching car slowed down and the flashing red beacon lit up on its roof. Betty's heart sank.

No one got out of the police car for a moment, then both front doors opened at once and a pair of uniformed troopers got out of either side.

"Oh, officers," she blurted, "I'm so glad to see you. I've had an accident."

"Elizabeth Krasicki?" the taller of the two, the one who'd been driving said. As he did, his partner unsnapped his holster.

Betty's eyes got the look she'd seen on the deer. "Uh —uh –"

The trooper stepped closer. "We have orders to detain you, Miss."

Betty's hand dipped into her pocket, but in the headlights of the police car, she saw the second trooper's gun drawn and pointed at her. She froze, and a hand clamped on her wrist. The trooper took the pistol from Betty and handed it to his partner, who dropped the clip and worked the slide. "Empty."

Betty's eyes popped wide.

"You're a very lucky woman, Miss. If that gun cleared your pocket, you'd be dead right now." His partner cuffed her hands behind her back.

Betty kicked and struggled, but it was no use. As the troopers were loading her into of their car, headlights came from behind.

"Cops," Shimmy eased off the gas at the sight of the spinner. "Oh, hell."

"What?"

"It's Betty's car."

They passed as Betty disappeared into the back of the cruiser. Shimmy groaned. "The Boss'll go bananas."

"So we shoot 'em and take the broad," Tuds said, reaching for his piece.

Shimmy cracked the gas and accelerated away. "Now I know you're crazy. One of 'em, maybe, but two? No way."

"So what do we do?"

"Right now, I'm going to find a pay phone and call the Bunny. This is news I don't want to deliver in person. And then I'll decide whether to just keep driving."

(20)

Fowler had Kendall drop him at his office and he'd take a cab home. He signed in at the lobby and the officer at the desk said, "You're popular tonight."

"Oh yeah?"

"People been asking for you the last half hour."

Fowler shrugged. "I'm here now."

Fowler took the elevator upstairs and on his desk, he found three reports and a half dozen memos.

The first report was from Cooper. It was twelve pages long and pretty much a rehash of the details of the robbery. Not much news. The second was the autopsy report for Metzler. The janitor died of asphyxiation caused by a crushed larynx. Again no surprises.

The third report was Krajovic's autopsy. A note was clipped to it, written in the nearly illegible scrawl of the medical examiner: PAGE FOUR — IMPORTANT.

Fowler flipped through the stapled sheets. On four, a sentence was underlined and tagged with an asterisk: "Water from the subject's lungs contains chlorine consistent with city tap water and chemicals found in cleaning solvents."

Fowler whistled a low note. Krajovic didn't drown in the Potomac. He was drowned in his mop bucket, and someone went to a lot of trouble to drag his body through the pipe chase to throw it in the river. The thieves left Metzler and the dead guards. Why take Krajovic, except to throw them off the trail?

As big and strong as Krajovic was, it must have taken a real monster to hold his head in a bucket.

He thumbed through the memos. Call Cooper. Call Cooper. Call Cooper. He looked at his watch. Cooper could wait until tomorrow. For that matter, so could calling Kendall. Krajovic would be just as dead in the morning.

4

On his desk, Fowler found three reports...

He decided to wait to call Sally too. Better to not make a personal call on a Bureau phone, especially to a co–worker. Fowler was reaching for the phone to call a taxi when it rang.

"Fowler."

"Call for you from the Virginia State Police."

He jiggled the hook and said, "Agent Fowler."

"This is Sergeant Malloy from Barracks C in Kensington. I have a note to alert you about an APB subject we have in custody, Elizabeth Krasicki. We're holding her here."

"That's good news, Sergeant. We'll be there in the morning to pick her up. You can hold her uncharged for twenty-four hours."

"Longer than that. She tried to draw down on two troopers. We'll make her comfortable."

"Thank you, Sergeant."

"Always glad to cooperate with the Bureau."

Fowler clucked his tongue. The perils of dealing with a woman in love.

When he got to his apartment, Fowler hung up his suit jacket, took off his necktie, poured two fingers of Scotch, and dialed Sally's number. She picked up on the second ring.

"Hello?" No sleep in her voice.

"Hi, Sally."

"Dan." Her voice reflected pique and relief at the same time. "Took you long enough to call. I was starting to worry."

"Hot on the trail, honey. You know how that is."

"Why couldn't we be something more sensible —like newspaper reporters?"

Fowler snorted. "Almost as dangerous, but no gun to shoot back."

"How's the case coming?"

"You know, slow but steady wins the race. Gotta follow the path one step at a time. Sorry about supper tonight. Can we try for tomorrow?"

Sally laughed. "I'll check my calendar."

"Do that. I'll talk with you in the morning."

"Get some sleep. You're going to need it."

Tito picked up his office chair and threw it over his desk to crash into the wall. "Aaugh! Jesus God! What else can go wrong?" Pug, accustomed to his boss's temper, ignored the rhetorical question and picked up the chair, righted it, and put it behind the desk.

"Stroud, that tail-chasing idiot; this is all his fault. Him and that brainless bimbo. The plan was perfect. And they've screwed it up! I'll kill them both!" He leaned on his desk, gripping the edge, white–knuckled. He waited 'til his breath slowed before he spoke again.

"That Fowler. I want him dead too. He's too smart for his own good."

"I don't know, boss. Whacking a Fed might bring on more heat."

"Fowler is the heat." Tito snapped and sank into his chair. He stared at his desk blotter for a moment then in a quieter voice, he told Pug, "Get out of here."

The plan was perfect. Steal the plates, smuggle them out of the country, and hand them to the Capo di Capo, who in turn would present them to Mussolini. Il Duce's crackdown on the Mafia in Sicily had been a thorn in the organization's side for a decade, jailing their principals and crippling their operations. But now, war as looming, and Mussolini and the Fascists needed money.

How better to demonstrate that Il Duce needed the cooperation of the Mob stateside and at home than to present him with a source of endless American dollars. The gift was symbolic, but it would show him that he wanted the Mob as allies, not adversaries, stateside and in Italia. And it wouldn't hurt Tito's status locally, doing a favor for the home team.

Tito ground his fist in his palm. I'll fix this, he thought, starting with Betty Mace and Stroud, and that meddling Fowler too. He'll be on a slab in no time, and the sooner the better.

(21)

In the morning, Fowler went to the office early, stopping at the news stand but not the diner.

He opened the Washington Times and scanned the headlines from masthead to tail. No mention of the BEP robbery and no mention of Krajovic or even a John Doe in the river. The Director had his hands on the press's collar for sure, but Fowler wondered how long he could keep the story quiet.

His first call was to Kendall, who answered on the third ring, yawning as he did. "Yeah?"

"It's Dan."

"What time is it?"

"Seven-thirty. We have an errand to run. The State Police have Betty Mace in custody. They're holding her for us at the Kensington barracks."

"Can't they bring her in?"

"The Director wants this kept as quiet as we can keep it. The fewer people involved, the less likely something will leak. Shall I pick you up?"

"I want to sign in at the office first before we get the lovely Miss Krasciki. I'll meet you there."

Time to call Cooper. He dialed the number and waited for the switchboard to connect him.

"Cooper."

"Fowler here."

"Why haven't you returned my calls?" On the phone, Cooper sounded like a cranky old woman. "We need to work together on this. You can't expect results if you keep me in the dark."

"I've been out of the office working the case. You don't catch bad guys sitting at your desk. What do you have for me?"

"I was about to ask you the same question,"

"Based on that comment, I'd say you've got zip."

Silence for a moment. "Not much. We found prints from the janitors all over, but we would have anyway. No mystery prints. This was a very professional job. We did find one thing, though. Under a dead guard's body we found a slip of paper. It was office stationery, a memo from Jenkins the building manager. It says Savage was walking a new man through the night rounds. Name's George Wilson.

"I checked it out. Totally bogus. No record of anyone by that name; not even an interview or application."

"Clever boys."

"They seem to have anticipated every contingency. It's locking the barn after the horse is stolen, but we've put out a general memo for everyone to lock up their letterhead. Savage cleaned Jenkins' office every night. It was easy access,"

"So they brought in at least one outsider. That widens the scope."

"Now, Fowler, what've you got?"

He thought about it for a minute, weighing how much to tell Cooper over the phone. "First, you won't read about it for a day or two, but Krajovic's out of the game. He turned up swimming with the swans. So, now it's down to Stroud and Savage."

"A falling out among thieves?"

"Or the elimination of a patsy."

"No word on Stroud or Savage?"

"Nothing so far from the APBs on those two yet, but the State Police have Stroud's girlfriend on ice on a different charge. We'll pick her up today. Right now, we're hoping she'll lead us to Stroud. We're following a few other leads, but they haven't panned out yet."

Cooper huffed. "That's just great. My boss says the White House is on his neck, and it all flows downhill."

"Your boss and mine. We're checking out potential connections between Stroud and a mobster named Marcoletto, but so far, nothing solid. Here's a thought; if Savage got the outsider close enough to the guard to break his neck, he had to be wearing a work suit and have an ID badge. BEP people wear photo IDs, right?"

"Yes."

"You do them onsite?"

"Yes, we do."

"Check the camera and the darkroom. Maybe they were careless."

"All right."

"And I'll let you know what we get from Stroud's lady friend."

"Please do."
Fowler hung up.

Shorty Dunlevy opened the padlock on his junkyard gate; Dunlevy's Auto Salvage, three acres of rusting wrecks. The sun was up, and the sky was blue. Shorty was sweating already in the humid July air.

Movement caught his eye from the southwest corner of the lot. Birds. Crows to be specific.

"Oh, hell," he said. "Hope it ain't one of my dogs." Shorty whistled and from the corners of the lot the mongrels came bounding. They rubbed against the legs of his coverall, eager for breakfast.

"Three, four, five." All there. "Better go see what them crows're peckin' at," and to the dogs, "You killed it, you'll eat it."

As he threaded his way through the ranks of bad drivers' mistakes, he saw the center of activity was a totaled Pontiac coupe. The birds were wheeling around the trunk lid, which was slightly ajar.

Shorty flapped his arms, sending the birds squawking in an angry mass. What was it you called a bunch of crows? Not a flock —a murder —that was it. His wife always said he wasted his time doing crossword puzzles, but that was one way to learn stuff.

He tugged at the handle of the trunk, and the lid groaned open.

A corpse was jammed into the compartment. Its eyes stared into the sky, and its slit throat gaped like a second smile.

Shorty gagged and puked down the front of his coverall and sat down hard on the packed earth.

The crows came back. Shorty didn't bother to shoo them away.

Five minutes later, Larry came in.

"Anything new?"

"Not much. Cooper has nothing. The Director's kept the whole business out of the papers for now, but it can't last long in this town."

"You never know. The Jastrenzky case hasn't seen the light of day yet."

"Don't even say that name out loud. You have a point, but that was strictly Bureau involvement. We didn't have Treasury and D.C. Homicide mucking around in the middle of things."

"Right. Three can keep a secret if two of them are dead."

"Benjamin Franklin spoke the truth."

On the way out of the building, they saw Plug Sandrock standing on the sidewalk, arms akimbo. Another man in a suit stood beside him.

"Now, Daniels, here you see a fine example of our tax dollars at work. Fowler, Kendall, this is Arvin Daniels from the D.A.'s office. He wants to talk to you about a certain corpus delecti you mugs 'borrowed' from the City Morgue."

"You're interfering with a homicide investigation," Daniels said. "I have a court order here for you two to return the body of one William Krajovic immediately, signed by Judge Warburton."

"Let's not get into a pissing contest, Plug," Kendall said. "You're aimed into the wind. Our judges trump yours every day."

"You guys think you're such hot shit. You may be Feds, but out here, you're standing on my sidewalk."

Fowler raised a restraining hand. "Take it easy. You can have the body, Plug. We're done with it. Just take your order to the clerk on the second floor,"

Kendall chuckled.

Plug glared at him. "I'm watching you two." He pointed a finger at Kendall. "Your day'll come, smart guy, and then it'll be my turn to laugh."

"One of life's few pleasures that doesn't cost a nickel." Fowler touched the brim of his hat with two fingers. "Nice meeting you, Counselor."

As they walked to the car, Fowler said. "Sandrock'd be a good cop if he just learned the politics of the pecking order."

"Everybody wants to be us."

"They should be careful what they wish for."

"We taking my car?"

"Can't use what the Bureau gave me, unless we put Betty in the rumble seat. I'll park it in the motor pool garage. Pick me up there."

(22)

The holding area of the Kensington State Police barracks was a row of cinder block cells with simple fixtures. Betty Mace sat on the shelf that served as a bunk, clutching her knees to her chest. She wore an ill-fitting set of prison grays. Her breakfast tray sat untouched, the coffee cold. Jimmy, oh, Jimmy, she thought. I've screwed up big time. Another fifteen minutes and I've made it. If it wasn't for that damned deer.

Down the corridor, the barred door slid open. Footsteps.

A uniformed sergeant, a matron holding her street clothes, and two guys in suits. She recognized the FBI agents who came to the Bunny the night before.

The trooper unlocked the cell and slid the barred door aside. "Miss Krasicki, these men are Federal agents. We're releasing you to their custody."

Betty glared at Fowler and Kendall. "I want a lawyer."

Kendall smiled. "All in good time, Betty."

The matron stepped into the cell and handed Betty the clothing.

"Where's my purse? And my jewelry?"

"They'll be returned at the desk when you're released," the sergeant said.

"We'll leave you with the matron to change clothes."

"Why bother?"

Betty grabbed her shirt in both hands and yanked it open, sending buttons flying across the cell. They clattered on the concrete floor. The sergeant was goggle-eyed at the sight of her breasts. Fowler and Kendall were impassive.

"Saw it all last night, Betty," Kendall said.

"Kiss my ass." For emphasis, she turned her back on them and pulled down the trousers. The matron grabbed the blanket from the bunk and held it as a makeshift screen.

"Fiesty isn't she?" the sergeant said.

"It's a professional posture."

In a few minutes, Betty walked out of the barracks between the agents into the hot morning sun. "Where are you taking me?"

"Back home to D.C.," Fowler said, "unless of course you want to take us where you were going last night when you hit that deer."

Betty spat in his face.

As Fowler wiped his cheek with a handkerchief. Kendall said, "I'd take that as a no."

They bundled Betty into the back of Kendall's car and cuffed her to the door handle. "Apologies, Betty. Procedure. Can't have you jumping out at a stop light. Just think of it as a new piece of jewelery."

On the ride back, Betty sat, sullen and unspeaking. The agents talked about anything that came to mind; baseball, economic recovery, golf. Betty was desperate, but a plan was forming in her mind. She'd fix these smug sons of bitches.

Sheriff Clete Brennan stood, arms akimbo looking at the corpse in the back of the Pontiac. No one had been murdered in his jurisdiction since Sadie Barnes poisoned her abusive, cheating husband. He'd called the coroner and they were sending the wagon to pick up the body.

Smitty, the deputy pulled a piece of paper from his pocket and unfolded it. He studied it for a minute, looked at the corpse then back to the paper. He leaned in for a closer look.

"What?"

"I dunno, Clete. This picture's kinda fuzzy, but I think our friend here looks like this fellow from the APB we got yesterday."

"Are you serious?"

"Hell, yeah. He held out the paper, which had the BEP photos of Stroud, Savage and Krajovic. "This one in the middle, Savage. See that little notch in his nose —left side —it's him. I'd bet my pay on it."

Brennan stared at the photo then back to the corpse. "I think you're right,

Smitty." He squinted his eyes and read the phone number at the bottom of the page. He turned to Shorty. "I gotta use your phone."

They were halfway to headquarters when Kendall stopped for gas at an Esso station. The pump jockey, a grizzled old man, shirtless in overalls came around the side of the car to fill the tank.

"Do you have a pay phone here?" Fowler asked him.

He shook his head. "No phone at all."

"Fill it up."

Betty figured this was her chance. She ripped the front of her dress and started to scream.

"Help! Help! I'm being kidnapped! Call the police!"

The old man froze, staring through the back window at Betty. Fowler opened his jacket to pull out his badge and the old man saw his gun. He put up a hand, palm open. "Don't hurt me, mister. I ain't seen nothin'. I ain't heard nothin'."

"Easy, old timer. We're Federal agents." He flashed his badge and handed the old man a business card. "I'm Special Investigator Fowler. My partner and I are transporting a prisoner."

Betty kept screaming and pounded on the window. He looked skeptical. "What'd she do?"

"She pulled a gun on two State Troopers, for a start. She's also a material witness in a homicide and robbery."

He still looked unconvinced but relieved to have an excuse to let it drop. He went back to cranking the pump handle, ignoring Betty's protests.

"That'll be two dollars thirty cents."

Fowler gave him three singles. "Keep the change."

As they drove away, in the rearview mirror Kendall could see him standing by the pump, staring after them. He chuckled. "Nice try, Betty. Never underestimate the power of the badge."

Betty swore under her breath.

"What did she say, Larry?"

" Something you shouldn't repeat in front of a lady,"

"Watch for a pay phone. I want to call the office."

"You got it."

When he got to a phone, Fowler had the operator retrieve his messages. Call Cooper, call Cooper, and a message to call Sheriff Clete Brennan of Sussex County concerning the APB on Arthur Savage. Fowler dialed O and the operator told him, "Thirty-five cents for the first two minutes."

He fished in his pocket for the change and dropped it into the phone. It clanged and clanked into the box, and in a moment, Fowler could hear the familiar buzz as it rang at the other end.

A gruff voice answered. "Sussex County Sheriff's Office."

"This is Special Investigator Daniel Fowler of the FBI. May I speak with Sheriff Brennan?"

"You got him. I'm Brennan."

"You called the Bureau about our fugitive Arthur Savage."

"I think we got him for you."

"You think?"

"Looks like him, but somebody needs to make a positive I.D."

"So you're holding him?"

"No need. He ain't goin' anywhere. Coroner's got him in a drawer at the Morgue."

Fowler hung up the phone and walked back to the car. He waved Larry out of the car so he could talk without Betty hearing him. "Change of plans, Larry. We're making a side trip. The Sussex County Sheriff thinks they've found Savage —dead."

Kendall whistled. "These boys play for keeps."

"If it is Savage. We need a positive identification, and I'm betting our prisoner can do that for us. My guess is she's met him hanging around with Stroud."

"One way to find out."

"It might shock her into compliance."

"Yeah, but it would be brutal."

"But we will do it, won't we?"

"Have to."

Fowler shook his head. "We are bastards, aren't we?"

"Takes one to catch one, Danny boy."

Three miles further, they reached a crossroad. Kendall turned left.

"Hey!" Betty yelled. "This isn't the way to D.C. Where the hell are you taking me?"

"Quick study, isn't she?" Kendall said,

"Sure is. Sorry, Betty. We have a little side trip to make. Bureau business. Just sit back and enjoy the ride."

(23)

Stroud sat at the table in the main room of the hideout. Tuds sat across from him playing solitaire. Barstow was lying down in one of the bedrooms. The doc had been back to check on him and found he had a fever. He gave Barstow a shot and said he should take it easy if he was going to be ready to travel on the twenty-third.

Shimmy had left a half hour before, saying he was going to a phone to check in with the boss. Neither he nor Tuds said why they were there or what was going on, and it made Stroud nervous. He tried small talk, but it went nowhere. Shimmy and Tuds were nervous too, and that didn't worry Stroud, it terrified him.

The whole deal looked great at the start; steal the plates from the BEP, take the money and run. Hide out in Mexico, where he could live for practically nothing for a while til the market recovered and buy in again. It was sweet; Marcoletto put him on his payroll and treated him like a king. And he gave Stroud his choice of the girls from the Bunny. Stroud chose Betty.

But, as sometimes happens, love got in the middle of things. Betty fell for him, hard, and started talking about the future. He liked her a lot. She was a real looker, and knew tricks in bed that would amaze Cassanova, but a permanent dame wasn't part of his plan. He played along with it to keep her happy, but once he got Pouch on the ship, he was gone.

Another reason he didn't want to shake the tree was sitting in front if him. He'd seen Tuds kill two people and didn't want anyone thinking he wasn't a hundred percent on board. Tuds could kill him with one hand while he poured himself a drink with the other. He'd seen Tito lose his temper, too, and didn't want to have it aimed his way. No way was Stroud going to say or do anything to make Marcoletto say the word.

"Damn!" Tuds slammed his hand on the table, making the glasses and bottles dance. Stroud jumped too. "Black ten stuck under the red jack, or I'd'a won."

Stroud was about to say there was always another game but the look on Tuds' face warned him away. Looking in his eyes, Stroud could see the ferris wheels and merry-go-rounds spinning inside the killer's skull.

Jefferson was the Sussex County seat and a quiet contrast to the bustle of D.C. "Not a bad place to raise a family," Kendall said.

"Yeah for somebody else. I can't picture you with a wife and a couple of brats, Don Juan."

"Hey, you never know. The right woman may come along some day." He pointed. "There's the Sheriff's office."

Kendall parked in front of a two-story brick building with a simple sign in the narrow patch of grass out front: COUNTY LAW ENFORCEMENT OFFICE CLETUS BRENNAN, SHERIFF. The sign was weathered but the name less so, painted over a number of Brennan's predecessors.

"I'll go in, Larry. You stay here in case Betty gets conversational."

Fowler found Sheriff Brennan at his desk, tipped back in his swivel chair, a fan blowing on his bare chest. His khaki uniform shirt hung on the coat tree along with his hat, both dark with sweat stains. Brennan was bulky, like an old football player starting to go to fat. He had a farmer's suntan, from the biceps down and the collarbone up.

"I apologize for the informality, Agent Fowler," he said, rising from his chair. "It's just so damned hot today."

Shaking Brennan's hand was like squeezing a two-by-four. "No problem, Sheriff. I have to give you credit for spotting our fugitive, assuming it's him."

"Oh, I can't take credit for that. My deputy Smitty studies every poster and alert comes in here. He saw the resemblance." Brennan retrieved his shirt, and as he buttoned it, he said. "Why you after this fella? If I may ask."

"Robbery." Fowler didn't elaborate, and Brennan took the hint. He put his short brimmed Stetson on his head and said, "Let's go see the Coroner. He's right down the street."

They picked up Kendall and Betty on the way. Kendall took the cuff from the door handle and snapped it onto his wrist. "Don't worry, Betty" he said with a chuckle. "This doesn't mean we're engaged or anything."

Brennan's eyebrows raised.

"Material witness." Kendall said. "C'mon, Betty."

The Coroner's office was in the basement of the court house, an imposing pile of granite that resembled a medieval fortress. The temperature dropped palpably as they descended the stone steps to the lower level.

"You ought to move your office down here, Sheriff."

"You might have something there, Fowler."

The basement level was arranged around a twenty-by-twenty area in the center with rooms branching off in all directions. The center area was piled with crates and boxes. At the far end they saw a door with the words ELLIS PAYNE COUNTY CORONER on the glass.

A wiry little man in a collarless shirt and suspenders sat behind a desk piled with papers and files. He looked up as they entered, and Fowler was startled at the look of his pale blue eyes, magnified by rimless spectacles that were barely noticeable, making his exaggerated eyes look grotesquely natural.

"Ellis, these fellows are FBI. They want a look at the body we brought in today."

Payne rose from the desk, and as he crossed the office to a connecting door marked Morgue, Fowler noticed a pronounced limp. Payne saw him looking and said, "Argonne. A Jerry buzz bomb hit our medical tent. I had to tie a tourniquet to my own leg. He rapped on it with his knuckles. Now it's hickory from the knee down. You two are young enough to have missed the War. Consider yourselves lucky."

"There's always another one," Kendall said.

"Isn't that the truth."

They followed Payne into the morgue, a small but efficiently arranged room with a pair of enameled examination tables positioned over drains. Cabinets held bottles of chemicals. Surgical saws and other heavier tools of the trade hung from hooks on the wall. A pair of three drawer cabinets sat side by side like a double dresser.

The acrid scent of formaldehyde stung Fowler's nose.

A tall man in a stained lab coat was scrubbing a steel pan in the slop sink. "Elroy," Payne said, "Pull out number four." He turned to the agents. "I haven't done the autopsy yet, but the cause of death is pretty obvious."

Elroy pulled out the drawer, revealing a body under a shroud. Fowler turned back a corner of the sheet, studied the face of the corpse then covered it again. He nodded to Kendall, who pulled Betty over. Without a word, Fowler yanked the sheet away. Betty gasped and whispered, "Arthur."

Betty was lucky she'd passed on breakfast. Bile rose in her throat and she gagged but didn't vomit.

"Now, Betty, you see what kind of people your boyfriend's playing with." Fowler said. "Take her out of here." Then to Payne, "Thank, you, Doctor. We'll arrange for transport of the body."

Back on the road, Betty was quiet for a few miles then she said, "Turn this goddamned car around."

(24)

The drive back to the city was tense. Shimmy drove with Tuds beside him. Stroud sat in the back seat with Pouch, who kept dozing off and falling against him. The courier was feverish, and from time mumbled incoherently.

"He's in a bad way," Stroud said. "He needs a doctor," to which Shimmy replied, "That's up to the Boss."

"But he's burning up," Stroud insisted.

Tuds turned his head slowly to lock eyes with Stroud. "Like he said, it's up to the Boss," closing the subject.

Stroud turned away from the drooling invalid and stared out the window at the passing scenery, wondering whether he'd live til the end of the day.

It was almost one when two green cars pulled into the gravel parking lot of a road house a half mile from Marcoletto's hideout and parked beside Kendall's Buick, where Fowler sat in the driver's seat with the door open, fanning himself with his hat. Betty sat in the back.

A tall, broad shouldered agent with close–cropped blonde hair approached the car.

"Agent Woods," Fowler said, "welcome to the party."

Woods nodded. "Fowler. What's the story?"

"A straight up knockover. A cabin in the woods. Kendall is casing it now. Follow me."

Fowler started the engine and the cars pulled onto the road in a line.

From the back, Betty said, "You'll keep your word? You won't hurt Jimmy?"

"I promise you, Betty, I'll do everything I can to keep him breathing."

Fowler led the raiding party to a clearing a half mile from the lodge. Six agents got out of the cars and began unloading long guns, bullet proof vests and other gear. Betty saw the rifles and shotguns and began to sob.

Woods opened a wooden chest and pulled out gas masks. He handed one to Fowler. As he did, Kendall stepped into the clearing.

"What's the word, Larry?"

"It's a cracker box. Front door, back door, two windows a wall. Plenty of brush and trees for cover except at the front where there's about a twenty foot clearing."

"Any movement?"

"I couldn't see inside. Blinds are pulled down. Nobody in or out. There are no cars around, but that doesn't mean anything. They may be parked somewhere nearby. No smoke from the chimneys or the stovepipe. Nobody came out while I was watching."

"What do you suggest, Larry?"

"Come in from east, south and west; two men in the brush out front to cover the door. Enter from the back."

"Tear gas?" Woods said.

"Not a bad idea. It'll keep anybody in there from shooting straight."

Woods turned to his team. "Masks, everybody."

"And remember, we want anybody we find in there taken alive, if possible." Fowler said that for Betty's benefit. She was leaning half out of the car, straining to hear.

Kendall nodded. "Whoever might be in there's a small fish. We want the big one, and dead men can't snitch." Fowler left one man to watch Betty, and the team deployed to take their positions. The dense forest made cover simple. Fowler and Kendall crouched on the south side, ready to rush the back of the lodge. Kendall kept an eye on his watch. "Three seconds, two, one." He pulled down his mask. "Time."

On the mark, tear gas canisters crashed through windows from all four sides. In seconds, the lodge was filled with choking fumes. The agents stood ready, adrenaline pumping, waiting for their quarry to run outside, but nothing happened.

Fowler signaled and the team converged from the woods, cautiously, guns at the ready. No movement nor sound came from the house. Fowler led his men onto the narrow back porch. They took positions on either side of the door.

It was fairly solid, and it took two kicks, not one, to splinter the frame. The agents swiveled into the open doorway, aiming riot guns into the kitchen. They swept the room quickly. No one. Fowler ran through the kitchen into the hearth room.

"Clear!"

The other agents ran behind him, dashing into the rooms on either hand through the billows of smoke. In a moment the lodge was cleared. Kendall came behind Fowler. "Nobody home," he said, his voice muffled by the gas mask. "Betty'll be disappointed."

"But they were here." Fowler plucked a cigarette butt from the ashtray in the middle of the table. He held it up. "Three rings. Stroud's brand. I count five more.""

"Progress."

"At this stage, I'll take what I can get, Larry."

Woods ordered his men to open the windows to air out the building. "Now what?" He asked Fowler.

"We search this place up and down."

"Do we have a warrant?"

"It'll be waiting for us when we get back to D.C. Take the place apart."

In a few minutes the air cleared and Fowler pulled off his gas mask. He wrinkled his nose at the lingering odor and wiped a sheen of sweat from his forehead with his sleeve.

The team was methodically going through every closet, cupboard, and drawer.

"Agent Fowler," one of the agents said, "You need to see this."

One of the bedrooms was outfitted as an infirmary, complete with a hospital bed. An enameled table held an array of surgical instruments laid out on a towel; on the bedside stand, a group of medicine bottles and hypodermic syringes. Flies buzzed around a waste can containing gauze spotted with blood and greenish–yellow pus near the bed.

"Somebody had some heavy treatment here, and not long ago." Kendall wrinkled his nose at the sharp odor of decay mixed with disinfectant.

Fowler leaned in to read the labels on the medicine bottles. "Morphine, penicillin, Prontosil –"

"Prontosil? I never heard of that one."

"It's new, German. Antibiotic."

Kendall grunted. He patted the pillow. "Whoever he is, he has a hell of a fever. The bed's still damp from him sweating. Was anybody shot at BEP?"

"Not according to Cooper. None of the guards even pulled a weapon, let alone fired it."

"So —what? They shot one of their own?"

"These people have a track record of eliminating accomplices; Krajovic, Savage. Maybe they did."

"But then why doctor him after the fact?"

"Good question. Answer that one, and maybe this whole business will make more sense."

Kendall crouched and rooted in the wastebasket with his fountain pen. "Maybe he wasn't shot." He stood and dumped the wastebasket on the bed. "Look at that, and that, and that," he said, pointing with the pen. "Unless somebody was sewing tents in here, those are suturing threads. Lots of them."

"Surgery?"

"Looks like it. At two tag ends per suture, I'd say at least forty stitches, maybe fifty."

"He must have a fever. The bed's still damp from him sweating."

"Sounds less like a gunshot every minute."

"One more mystery."

"Let's go break the news to Betty. This ups the ante.. Maybe she'll tell us more."

"But first, let's see what the team found."

(25)

Stroud had been in Marcoletto's headquarters in the warehouse beside the Bunny twice before. The first time was when Tito made him the offer to work the inside with Savage. The second was when Tito introduced him to Betty.

This wasn't such an auspicious occasion. Shimmy had pulled the car into the warehouse, and when they got out, Pug was waiting for them. "Upstairs."

Pug led them up the narrow stairwell, Shimmy in the lead followed by Stroud and Pouch with Tuds bringing up the rear. Pouch was having a bad time. He was out of breath halfway up, and his knuckles were white gripping the banister.

At the top, the door to Tito's office opened onto a tight landing, too small to swing a battering ram. The door was steel laminated with wood to look ordinary, but it would take a stick of dynamite to blow it down. Anyone who tried to shoot through it would hit himself with a ricochet.

Pug gave the knock and didn't wait for a response. He opened the door and ushered them inside. Tito sat at his desk, hands flat on the green blotter on either side of a snub nosed revolver and one bullet.

"Boss," Shimmy said, "We –"

"Shut up." No shouting, instead a voice that exuded cold rage. "You and I are gonna talk later. Right now, I wanna have a chat with Lover Boy." He stared at Stroud, his face flushed with anger, making the knife scar down his cheek stand out bright white.

"You've caused me a problem, Jimmy. I don't like problems. Starting now, you and the skirt are over."

"Mister Marcoletto, I–"

Tito raised a palm. "Just listen, No talk. You and the broad, no calls, no contact, nothing. Over. *Finito, capisce?*"

Stroud gulped. "Yes, sir."

Tito picked up the revolver and flicked out its empty cylinder. "You know, you can be replaced." He slipped the bullet into it. He snapped the cylinder into the frame and spun it. "Let's see if it's necessary."

Tito aimed the gun at Stroud's chest and pulled the trigger. Stroud cried out and started back as the hammer fell on an empty chamber.

"Not today. Maybe we'll try again tomorrow."

Stroud felt a wave of nausea wash over him, but it was Pouch who started to sag. Tuds caught him by a handful of his jacket and held him perpendicular.

Tito turned to Pug. "Get these idiots out of here before I kill all four of them." He pointed to the Pouch. "And get that rummy doctor here for him."

Doc Macon had problems of his own at the moment. He was sitting in a chair in the hearth room of the lodge surrounded by Feds firing questions at him.

He had gone to the hideout to check on his patient. Pouch, as Tito called him, had an infection, and it was no surprise. Macon had never done anything like the implantation he did at Tito's request, and there was no telling how the man might react to having those six-inch slabs stuck under his skin. The steel plates were coated with paraffin, but nothing was perfect. One nick or even a pinhole could cause the problem.

He had his orders. Tito wanted him healthy by the twenty–third, or else. And Tito got what he wanted, or else.

Doc needed a drink, maybe two, badly. He had to squeeze the steering wheel to keep his hands from shaking. But he couldn't chance driving with a couple hits of gin down his gullet. He'd made that mistake before

He pulled into the clearing but wasn't surprised to see cars parked there. People came and went, and Macon knew better than to ask questions. In the back of one of the cars, he saw a head of blond hair. On second glance, he recognized Stroud's bimbo, the stripper. What the hell was she doing out here?

Doc got about five steps toward the car when he heard the ratchet of a pump shotgun and a voice that said, "Freeze!"

Macon laughed. "You must be new. I'm on the team, pal." He turned to stare over a .12 gauge muzzle into the eyes of a man who said, "FBI. Drop the bag and raise your hands. Now!"

And now, he sat in a chair watching agents tearing the lodge apart.

"His driver's license says his name is Samuel Macon," said Kendall. He rummaged in the black leather satchel. "Tools of the trade, Dan; stethoscope, head mirror, tongue depressors, doctor tools."

Fowler leaned forward into Macon's line of vision. "So tell, me, doctor," he said with sarcastic emphasis on the title, "exactly what do you do for Tito in there?" He jerked a thumb at the makeshift infirmary. "Pluck out an occasional bullet? Stitch up a knife wound? Clean him up when catches the clap from one of his strippers?"

Macon was silent. If he talked, Marcoletto would see him dead, and worse first. I could hold out, he thought. If I could just have a drink, I could handle whatever these flatfeet can dish out. Just one little drink.

"Look here, Dan." Kendall held the bag open and Fowler peered inside. At the bottom of the bag lay a half empty pint of Gordon's Gin. The agents shared a nod.

Kendall took out the gin bottle and Macon's eyes drifted toward it then snapped away,

"Our friend is sweating, Agent Fowler."

"So are you. It's hot as the hinges on the gates of Hell in here."

"But my hands aren't shaking." He uncorked the bottle and shook it gently in front of Macon's eyes, sloshing the gin and giving Macon a whiff of it. "Sure is a hot day. I'd say it's a thirsty day. Wouldn't you, Doc?"

He replaced the cork and set the bottle on the table beside the bag as Woods came to the kitchen doorway. "Gentlemen, would you come in here, please."

"Watch him," Fowler said to one of Woods' men. The look in Macon's eyes was one of need, but not yet desperation.

Out of Macon's earshot, Larry said. "He'll crack."

"But soon enough?"

"I'm counting on it."

In the kitchen, the china cupboard had been pulled away from the wall. Behind it, the lath and plaster had been cut away to expose open joists holding an assortment of long guns and even a Thompson submachine gun. "If there was any doubt," Woods said.

Fowler shook his head. "None. We just justified the warrant. Pull up every floorboard."

"Who knows?" Kendall said. "Maybe we'll find the Lindbergh baby and Judge Crater's body before the day's over."

Back in the hearth room, Macon stared at the gin bottle. His skin felt as if worms were crawling under it. Just one drink, that's all he needed. The bottle sat just out of reach, three feet away. Three feet, just thirty-six inches. The gin looked like liquid silver in the bottle.

Across the room, the agents were tearing the couch apart. And that Fed, Kendall the other one called him, taunting him with the bottle. Macon wanted to kill him.

Kendall came back and pulled up a chair. "Yeah, it's a hot day, Doc." Kendall set a glass on the table and poured two fingers of Gordon's. He swirled the gin in the glass. "Yeah, a thirsty day." He dipped his forefinger into the glass and put it on his tongue. He smacked his lips.

Macon's eyelid twitched. He hadn't said a word since they nabbed him, and he wouldn't, but God, how he needed a drink. Just one drink.

Kendall tipped his head back and drank the gin slowly. He sighed and set the glass down. "Yeah, that hit the spot. A thirsty day. Thirsty, thirsty –"

Macon let out a cry of rage and anguish and leapt out of his chair. Instead of grabbing for the bottle, his hand dove into the bag and came out with a wicked looking Lister knife. He swung the blade in a flashing arc. Kendall jerked back, knocking over his chair. The point of the knife narrowly missed his throat, grazing his knuckles as he raised a hand to shield himself. The agents reached for their pistols, and Kendall said, "No, don't shoot him. We need him to talk."

Macon slashed back and forth, and caught Kendall's forearm. He stepped in to thrust at Kendall, who caught the doctor's arm at the wrist and bicep and brought the elbow down the wrong way, full weight, over his knee. There was a sharp crack, Macon screamed, and the knife fell to stick in the floor.

Fowler rushed in. Macon lay on the floor clutching his arm, whimpering in pain.

"Not exactly what I had in mind, Larry."

"That could have gone better." He pulled back his cuff and saw blood seeping through his sleeve. "So much for this suit."

"But we have him now for sure," Fowler said, yanking the doctor to his feet and planting him in the chair. "Assaulting a Federal agent, attempted murder, and I bet he doesn't have a license to practice medicine, at least not anymore. I bet you really need a drink now, don't you, doctor?"

Fowler turned to Woods. "We'll take the prisoner with us. I want to take your car for the radio. I want warrants waiting when we get back. You can drive Kendall's car."

"It'll take weeks to dig up the ground around this place. Who knows what or who might be buried outside."

"It's a gift."

Betty sat in the back seat of the green car, baking in the midday heat. Sweat pooled in her eye sockets and dripped from her chin. Her mascara was forming dark rivulets at the corners of her eyes.

Damn those flatfeet, she thought, leaving me sweating in this ugly car handcuffed to the goddamned door handle. She was thirsty, hungry, and royally pissed off. How long were they going to leave her out here? And alone. That agent took the alky doctor and never came back.

She'd been around enough juicers to know that the doctor was in it deep from the few times she'd seen him. It was in his eyes, in the gin blossoms on his cheeks; even the way he moved his head, like his brain was water sloshing around, and he was afraid if he tipped his head the wrong way, it would leak out his ears.

Where were they? Did they find Jimmy? Was he all right? Then the thought hit her. What if they sweated the doc and he told them what they wanted to know? Then they wouldn't need her and she'd have no leverage to help Jimmy or herself.

Voices. She looked over her shoulder. Fowler and Kendall were hauling the doctor down the path, one on a side. The doctor had his arm in a sling, and puke down the front of his shirt. These boys play rough, Betty thought.

As they approached the car, Betty said, "Jimmy! Where's Jimmy? Is he all right?"

"Jimmy wasn't there, Betty. Nobody was. But the good news is we didn't find his body, either."

Betty stared as Kendall wrestled the groaning prisoner into the back seat and cuffed his ankle to a ring mounted in the floor. "Here's some company for you, Betty. Since you didn't ask who he is, I figure introductions aren't necessary."

"I'll tell you everything I know!" Betty blurted out.

"Shut up, you bitch!" Macon lunged at Betty and she half fell out of the car dodging him.

"He speaks," Fowler said.

"Play nice, kids." Kendall grabbed the doctor by the shoulders and slammed him into the seat. Macon grunted in pain.

"Tell you what, Betty," Kendall said, uncuffing her, "Agent Fowler can ride back here with your buddy, and you can sit up front and tell me all about it."

Marcoletto paced back and forth in front of his desk. No word from Moon. That meant Fowler was still breathing.

Pouch had to board the Bella Maria for Italy in two days, and they'd never let him on the boat with that fever. If I have to, I'll put him on board in a crate, and that screw up Stroud with him. Or shoot him and ship his body in a coffin to the Old Country. Where in hell was the doctor?

A knock. Pug didn't wait for a response.

"Please tell me the doc showed up."

Pug shook his head. "Haven't found him yet. He wasn't at that flea bag where he lives, and we checked the joints where he hangs out. So far no luck. You want me to find somebody else?"

"Yeah. No. Don't. Another doctor might go to the cops. Give it another hour."

"Okay, boss." Pug closed the door behind him.

When this caper is over, Tito thought, I'm going to kill them all; Stroud, Betty, Macon, and those two screw-ups Shimmy and Tuds, and no matter what it takes or costs me, If Moon doesn't get get him, I'm going to personally put a bullet between that Fed Fowler's eyes.

(26)

Kendall pulled the Bureau car to a rear entrance of the headquarters building and drove down a ramp into the basement level. "Come on Betty." Kendall didn't bother to cuff her but took her firmly by the elbow and steered her toward a pair of elevators. Over her shoulder, she watched Fowler haul the doctor out of the back of the sedan and take him in another direction.

Upstairs, Kendall signed in and took her to a room with no windows. The only furniture was a table and four chairs. The overhead light was encased in a metal grille. A four- by three-foot mirror was set into the plaster on one wall, and Betty knew what it was, a one-way glass. Let them watch her, she thought. She was used to it.

She turned toward the mirror and held the ripped placket of her dress shut. "Sorry, boys, no free shows."

Her appearance in the mirror startled her. Her makeup was a mess. Kendall let her have her purse after he dumped it out and made sure there was nothing in it she could use as a weapon. She spit in a handkerchief and rubbed off as much lipstick and mascara as she could.

In a few minutes she had her face looking as good as it was going to and she settled into one of the hard metal chairs to wait. And wait.

Finally, the door opened and Kendall came in with a red-haired woman carrying a briefcase. Her dress was a nice cut to show off her hourglass figure, and not cheap either. Working for the Feds must pay pretty well, she thought.

The woman set the case on the table and pulled out a wire bound stenographer's pad and three pencils.

"Betty, this is Miss Marsh. She'll be taking your statement. Just tell her in your own words what you told Agent Fowler and myself in the car."

"Well, I –"

"Just a moment, please." The steno flipped open the cover of the pad and made a note at the top of the first page. She turned to Fowler. "Deponent's name?"

"Elizabeth Krascicki." He spelled it. "AKA Betty Mace."

Miss Marsh wrote the information down and looked across the table at Betty. "Please speak clearly, Miss Krasicki. If I need something spelled or repeated, I will ask. Please do not nod or shake your head in response." She looked up at Kendall. "Agent? Are you ready?"

"Yes." Kendall took a chair beside the steno and turned to Betty. "State your name for the record."

"Elizabeth Krascicki."

"Raise your right hand, please. Do you swear that the information you're about to give is the truth, the whole truth, and nothing but the truth, so help you God?"

Betty rolled her eyes. "Sure."

"Tell us the story you told Agent Fowler and myself in the car. Leave nothing out."

For the next half hour, Betty recounted her relationship as an employee of Tito Marcoletto, how she met Jimmy Stroud, and how they became romantically involved. At that point, Kendall interrupted.

"Betty, please describe the location where you recently met with James Stroud and what you saw there."

"You were there. That shithole in the middle of nowhere."

Kendall grinned. "Could you be a little more specific about the location? For the record."

"Two hours out of the city off Route 48. Down a dirt road by a windmill and back in the woods. Jimmy called it a hunting lodge but it's just a glorified shack."

"And why did you go there?"

"I went there to see Jimmy, why do you think?" Her eyes flicked around the room. "How about you give me a cigarette?"

"I think that can be arranged." Kendall made a gesture to Miss Marsh and she laid down her pencil. He pulled out a deck of Chesterfields and shook one out. Betty took one and leaned in to the flame of Kendall's Zippo. Betty took a drag and made a face. "At least it's not a Camel." Kendall nodded and the steno picked up her pencil.

"Back on the record, Betty. Besides James Stroud, who else was present?"

"Different people. Guys who worked for Tito Marcoletto. I saw them hanging around the Bunny. That drunk doctor they brought in. And some guy who was his patient, I guess. He was weird looking. His skin just sagged on him like loose stockings. He had big patches of gauze taped on either side of his belly."

Through the looking glass, Fowler sat beside Macon. The doctor stared through the one way mirror as Betty gave her testimony.

The snakes were crawling all over his insides. He took in a breath and let it out in a series of shuddering puffs. His arm hurt like hell, but it was nothing compared to the pain in his gut.

"The race is on, Sam. Mind if I call you Sam? Whoever tells us what we want to know first gets the break with the Prosecutor." Fowler pointed toward Betty. "Right now, she's in the lead. Way in the lead. So what's it going to be?"

The snakes were crawling through his brain now, slithering through its convolutions and coiling around his sanity.

Fowler set a glass on the table in front of them. "Empty. But an empty glass is always filled with air, Doc. You might think spilling what you know's an empty glass, but turning State's evidence can buy you air to breathe for a long time."

Fowler set a second glass on the table. On the other side of the mirror, Betty was telling Kendall about things he told her as they lay in bed.

Fowler poured gin into one glass, then the other. "Deal's on the table, Doc." He raised a glass. "Shall we drink to it?"

Macon stared at the glass, through the mirror at Betty, her mouth running nonstop, and reached a trembling hand for the gin.

"So tell me, Doc what exactly did you do to this Pouch guy?"

The Director listened to every word Fowler reported without speaking. When he was finished, Fowler said, "Sir, the question becomes what is the priority? Recovering the plates, or taking down Marcoletto's organization?"

The Director stared at his folded hands for a moment. "What do you recommend, Agent Fowler?"

"I understand that recovery of the plates is a presidential mandate, but to do that, we have to locate the man they call Pouch first. It's obviously a code name, and it hasn't turned up in any AKA lists.

"If we go after Marcoletto, who looks good for this caper, we may find this courier, Pouch, in the same place. My advice would be to hit Marcoletto hard and do it soon."

The Director said, "Agent Woods and his team haven't found the plates out there, but they found enough incriminating evidence for a warrant to arrest Marcoletto and his whole crew on a variety of charges and to justify searching any premise he owns. We can take him down any time. Finding this man Pouch is the main objective. We may have only one chance at the courier. If you hit Marcoletto at the wrong time, we may miss him."

Fowler sat unspeaking. He had learned long before that pressing the Director was the wrong thing to do. The Director turned his head to the left for a moment, as if studying something projected on the office wall. When he turned his head back toward Fowler, he said, "Let's err on the side of caution. Set up surveillance on the night club and see who comes and goes. In the meantime, keep beating the bushes."

There was a pause.

"And Fowler . . . ."

"Yes, sir?"

"No D.C. cops. I want this operation strictly in-house. I don't want Marcoletto tipped off by some crooked flatfoot on his payroll."

"Yes, sir. Does that include Treasury?"

"Marcoletto's got protection from someone on an upper rung; city, state, or Federal. Otherwise, he wouldn't have been able to operate for this long. At this point, I don't trust anybody." The Director opened a file on his desk and began to read it.

Dismissed.

Kendall was waiting in the anteroom when Fowler left the Director's office. "What's the word?"

Fowler said grimly, "Time to call in the eyeballs."

It was five-thirty when Fowler left headquarters. There still was no word on the Stroud APB, and while Woods' team was digging up all sorts of interesting evidence of Marcoletto's wrongdoing, there was nothing pointing to Pouch's whereabouts.

Inquiries at City Hall led through a maze of corporations to Marcoletto's lieutenant Benno Coppolino as the titular owner of the Mainline Storage building. Kendall was working to locate architectural drawings of the Bunny and the warehouse.

Dan didn't have time to shower and shave. Sally would have to take him as is.

As he pulled away from the curb, a block behind him, Tommy Moon kicked the starter of the big Indian he straddled, pulled goggles over his eyes and slipped into the traffic. Tito Marcoletto's words still smoked in his ears: "Fix this, or I'll kill you myself." Lindstrom was an honest mistake, he thought, but Fowler, you won't get away this time.

(27)

Fowler rang Sally's doorbell as the clock on the tower down the street chimed six. She came to the door in a yellow sun dress with her hair pulled back inside a floppy white hat. She stood on tiptoe to give Dan a quick kiss and said, "I hope your wallet's full. I'm hungry." She grabbed her purse from a table beside the door and closed the door behind her.

"I made us reservations at the Blue Flame."

Her eyebrows shot up. "Am I dressed okay? Will they let me in the place in this outfit?"

Fowler eyed her up and down. "Honey, they'll sell tickets."

At the curb, Sally looked up the street. "Well, where is it?"

"Where is what?"

"The Big Ugly. The Bureaumobile."

"Right in front of you."

Sally stared at the Caddy, back to Fowler, back to the Caddy, and back to Fowler. "This car?"

"Courtesy of the Bureau Motor Pool; it used to be Handsome Johnny Marcolini's."

"That's good. I was worried. I was afraid the Blue Flame wouldn't let you park one of those ugly green sedans in their lot."

A few miles outside the city, the buildings fell away to open country. Sally ditched the hat and tied her hair behind her with a scarf. Fowler decided she had the right idea and tossed his fedora behind the seat.

Ten miles out, temptation got the best of Fowler, and he decided see what Handsome Johnny's Caddy could do. He pushed the accelerator and the V-8's drone rose to a snarl then a scream as the speedometer needle neared eighty-five. He looked over to Sally, who smiled and nodded. She was enjoying the speed.

Fowler weaved in and out of the traffic, passing cars and trucks in a blur. He'd driven plenty of fast cars, but the Caddy was an exotic mix of power and luxury. It was like driving his living room sofa at a hundred miles an hour. The wind rushed in his ears like the sound of a waterfall, but not quite loud enough to drown out the wail of a siren behind him.

He looked in his rearview mirror and saw a motorcycle cop on a big Indian hot on his tail. "Uh–oh," he said. "We've got company."

"Oh, just pull over and show him your badge. Tell him you're pursuing a fugitive or something."

"I suppose I should." Fowler eased off the gas and slowed to pull off into a wooded side road away from the traffic. He stopped on the berm and the cop rolled up behind him. Fowler stepped out of the car as the cop got off his motorcycle. He was wearing a peaked service cap, knee high brown boots, tan Jodhpurs, and a leather jacket and gloves in spite of the heat. His jaw was set and his eyebrows furrowed as he stepped toward the roadster.

"Good evening, officer," Fowler said. "I'm Inspector Daniel Fowler of the FBI. I'm going to reach for my shield."

"Your name's all the I.D. I need," the cop said. His hand dropped, and Fowler noticed his holster was unsnapped. His gun was out and on the way up before Fowler could blink. Two shots boomed, a bullet whizzed past Fowler's head, and the cop pitched backwards. Fowler turned and saw Sally holding her purse with a hand inside it. Smoke drifted from a hole in its bottom.

"His boots are the wrong color," she said, almost inaudible. "Virginia cycle cops wear black."

Fowler stepped over to the fake cop and kicked the pistol out of his reach. Blood was pooling under the body and soaking into the gravel. He wasn't moving.

Sally got out of the car and stared at the corpse. "Too bad you killed him," Fowler said. "I would have liked to ask who he was working for. Maybe somebody at headquarters can I.D. him. Let's put him in the rumble seat."

"You're kidding."

"We can't leave him here."

"I guess you're right."

"Quick, before somebody comes along and sees us."

Between the two of them, they wrestled the body into the back of the roadster without getting too much blood on them. Fowler scribbled the motorcycle's serial number and Highway Patrol registry in his notebook. Then he kick started the Indian and rode it fifty yards into the adjacent woods. He laid it over and covered it with some brush. He put up the convertible top before starting the car. "Let's not be an easy target. He might have a partner."

On the drive back to D.C. Sally was quiet for a long time, and Fowler respected her silence. Everyone dealt with killing someone in his, or in this case, her own way. He switched on the Caddy's radio and dialed in a big band station, letting it play softly.

Finally, Sally reached over and shut off the music. "Dan, does it ever bother you when you have to shoot someone?"

Fowler noted her distinction between "shoot" and "kill." He reached over and took her hand in his. "It's not your first, Sally."

"No, it's my second." She hugged herself. "I feel numb. I feel like I should cry, but I can't."

"To tell you the truth, Sally, I don't think about it at the time, but I do later. Usually if I'm shooting at some mug, he's shooting at me —or at my partner. The day I put somebody down and don't think about it, it's time to hand in my badge."

Sally nodded. "I acted on reflex. I was suspicious of his boots, and when he said what he did and went for his gun, I pulled the trigger. I wasn't going to let him shoot you."

"Good that you did. After he killed me, he would have killed you —leave no witnesses. His gun was a .45 automatic, not a service revolver. He was a pro, so don't waste any tears on him."

"I won't, but I'm still puzzled how he got on your tail in this car so fast."

"Like I said, he's a pro. Maybe he's been on the job a while and finally saw his chance. I have enough enemies that he might have been collecting an old debt for someone I put away."

"You're dangerous company, Fowler."

"So are you, Sally, but not always for the same reasons."

Fowler stopped at a service station to use the pay phone while Sally went into the rest room to wash the blood from her hands. It was after hours, but the Bureau switchboard answered twenty-four hours a day. "Federal Bureau of Investigation." The night operator was male.

"This is Inspector Daniel Fowler." He rattled off his badge number.

"Yes, sir," the operator said. "How may I connect your call?"

"Who's on the night desk?"

"Agent Barnes."

"Put me through to him, please."

Bill Barnes was pulling desk duty while he recuperated from a bullet to his shoulder he caught during a gambling raid in Jersey City.

"Operations," Barnes' gruff voice said. Fowler imagined the burly agent, bulging out of his suit, his crooked nose and hound dog eyes, fuming over having to sit still for eight hours at a clip.

"Barnes, this is Fowler."

"Yes, Inspector Fowler?" No familiarity in the office. The Director demanded strict protocol, even between friends on the telephone.

"I'm bringing a package to receiving."

"Mobile?"

"Negative."

"Estimated arrival?"

"Within an hour."

"Receiving will be ready."

The line went dead. He'd deliver the assassin's corpse to a drop outside D.C.

From there it would be taken to be autopsied and, Fowler hoped, identified. Sally came back to the car, looking more composed. "Did you reach headquarters?"

Fowler nodded. "They're expecting us."

He pulled back onto the road with a crunch of gravel under the tires. Night had fallen, and every pair of head lights behind them set Fowler's teeth on edge. They tried once, he thought. They'll try again.

"So, Dan," Sally said. "Tell me about this case you're working on."

As they drove, Fowler told her about the robbery and murders at the BEP Annex and the tandem investigation with Treasury.

"So who knew you and I were going out tonight?"

"Nobody but Larry. Looks as if someone was tailing me."

"That's what I think, too. Do you think they'll try again?"

"They won't have to try again. Benny's gonna kill me when he sees the mess in the trunk."

"So much for supper," Sally said. "I don't think I could eat right now anyway."

They were silent for a moment, then Fowler said, "And, Sally, thanks."

She nodded. "You're welcome. And do us both a favor."

"What's that?"

"Don't speed. I don't want to get pulled over again."

(28)

Fowler pulled up to the gate of a fenced-in warehouse just outside the city. He flashed his lights, and in a moment, a uniformed guard came from the cinder block building. Dan got out of the Cadillac and strode to the gate. He flashed his credentials. "I'm Inspector Fowler."

"Yes, sir. You're expected." The guard pulled the gate aside and waved Dan through it. A bay door rolled upward and Fowler could see an unmarked van inside with four men in coveralls standing beside it. He pulled the roadster in and the door rolled down behind him.

He recognized three of the four men inside from previous occasions. They would handle the fake cop's body from this point, taking it to the Bureau's pathologist for autopsy. There would be an official inquiry, but it would be at the Director's discretion pending identification of the shooter whether the death would ever be officially reported. In a world of secrets, the FBI had more than its share.

Fowler opened the rumble seat.

"What the hell?" Billings, the crew chief said. "A cop?"

"A fake one."

The team carefully lifted the body from the rumble seat and loaded it onto a stretcher. Billings held out a clipboard. "Sign here, Fowler."

"These go along too," Dan handed Sally's automatic and the gunman's, wrapped in a handkerchief to Billings.

He sniffed the muzzles. "Both fired."

"It was give and take."

"Congratulations."

"Not to me. Kudos to Agent Vane." He tilted his head toward Sally, who sat watching through the windshield. "It's her gun. If she hadn't acted, I'd be dead."

Billings gave a low whistle. "No kidding? Up to now, I had my doubts about female agents. Not anymore."

"There's a Highway Patrol motorcycle in the woods across the border in the next county, probably stolen like the uniform. I'll contact their office in the morning and they can retrieve it. I only hope the cop it belongs to is still breathing."

"Okay, Inspector Fowler. We'll take it from here."

The bay door rolled upward. Fowler backed the Caddy out and turned it around in the parking lot. In a moment, he and Sally were driving away from the drop.

"Dan, Sally said, with a touch of hesitancy in her voice, "I hope you don't think I'm being weird, but . . . "

"But what?"

I know I shouldn't be, but I'm hungry."

"Not weird at all. There have been plenty of times when I came close to being killed and was famished once the adrenaline wore off. Maybe looking Death in the face makes you feel more alive."

He let that thought sink in then said, "We lost our reservation at the Blue Flame, but Molly's is close."

She smiled for the first time since the shooting. "Sounds great. Let's do it."

"Yes, ma'am." Fowler put his foot on the gas and the Caddy zoomed away.

Molly's was one of those all–night diners built like a railroad car; booths and windows on one side of a narrow aisle, and stools and counter on the oth-er, the kitchen behind. It wasn't busy at the moment, and they were able to take a booth at the back. Sally slid across the cracked leather seat. Fowler thought twice and decided Sally might not want to be crowded, so he sat opposite her.

A waitress in a pink uniform and a snood over her hair ran up with a coffee carafe and a pair of cups and saucers. She set them down and started pouring the coffee. "Evening, folks. What'll you have?"

"How's the steak tonight?"

"The best T–bone in town, mister."

"Two of them medium rare, with home fries and green beans."

The waitress smirked and turned to Sally. "And you, Miss?"

Her joke broke the tension, and everyone laughed. Sally said, "We'll share."

"On the way." She headed for the kitchen, shouting ahead of her, "Two T-bones, Eddie!"

Sally shook her head. "I still think I should feel guilty."

"Don't. It's your reward for survival."

Fowler and Sally had to file separate incident reports, and Fowler spent a good part of his morning preparing his. He hadn't seen Sally that day because he didn't want any appearance of impropriety or collusion on their accounts of the shooting. He was about to send his handwritten manuscript to the typing pool when Larry Kendall leaned into the doorway.

"Got a positive I.D. on the gunman. Name's Tommy Moon. Ring any chimes?"

Fowler shook his head. "None. What's his pedigree?"

"Moon was a button man, originally from Pittsburgh. Five suspected hits, no convictions. I'd say Sally performed a public service taking him out." He sat in a chair opposite Fowler's desk. "How is she?"

"I don't know. I haven't seen her today. She was a little shaken last night, but she seemed okay."

"She's a tough cookie."

"And she saved my ass."

"Don't worry about her or her career. From what you told me, it was a justified kill."

"Yeah, I know that, but I'm worried that because she was with me, unofficially, the fraternization policy may kick in."

"I suppose that could factor into it."

"It could get us both in trouble, her worse than me. She's in a precarious spot to begin with, being one of the few female agents in the Bureau. She's worked hard to get where she is, and I don't want it to be for nothing."

It was late morning. The intercom buzzed. "Inspector Fowler," the metalic voice said, "The Director would like to see you."

"Now," Fowler added with a sigh. He stood. "Drop by later, Larry, I want to run some things past you about the case."

The Director stood, as he often did, staring out his office window at the street below. Dan entered the office and quietly closed the door. Neither spoke for a moment.

"Hell of a thing," the Director said. "A hit man disguised as a traffic cop. The

"Don't feel guilty. It's your reward for survival."

Highway Patrol says the Indian was stolen in Upton yesterday. The uniform is anyone's guess."

"That's what gave him away, sir. His boots."

The Director grunted. "Do you think this is related to your current case? Or was it some rival of Marcolini spotting the car and seeing an opportunity?"

"Doubtful it was one of Marcolini's enemies, sir. When I said my name, Moon said, and I quote, 'That's all the I.D. I need.' I was the target. And he didn't know me on sight."

"You're probably right." He turned and his eyes bored into Fowler. "But how did he get onto you so quickly?"

"That, I don't know, sir."

"When did you pick up the roadster?"

"Two mornings ago at about ten–thirty."

The Director opened a file folder on his desk to show a stark photograph of a dead man slumped over the steering wheel of a car, a bullet hole under his left ear. "This man, a Robert Lindstrom who worked for the Bureau as a file clerk, was shot yesterday in traffic not a hundred yards from this building." He slid the photo aside to reveal another of the same scene from a few yards away. "Recognize the car?"

It was a light colored Cadillac, a series 60 roadster.

"What time did this happen?"

"At four thirty."

"That can't be Marcolini's car. It was parked at the motor pool garage."

"It isn't. The car is registered to a Gustav Lindstrom, the victim's uncle. It could be a coincidence, Fowler, but we can't risk believing in coincidences. That young man was murdered in the same model and color car you were driving when you were pulled over by Tommy Moon, who tried to murder you. The young man was also your size and build. I say no coincidence."

"I agree, sir. If this were an old grudge, the party behind it would have had a positive visual I.D. So it was the car that the hitter used to identify me."

"Apparently. I've thought about pulling you off this case right now, Fowler, unless you can give me good reasons why I shouldn't."

"If I may, sir," Fowler said. "Assuming the two incidents are connected, which I believe to be true, whoever is behind it all has singled me out. The fact that they want me dead tells me that I'm getting close. I would respect-fully recommend that I be allowed to remain in the investigation in the hope of forcing their hand."

"I'm not in the habit of using my agents as bait, Fowler. However, in this case I agree with your thinking. These incidents hit too close to home, and if the leak is in the Bureau, I need to know, and to plug it permanently. Stay with it for now, and I expect a daily report from you."

"Yes, sir."

"And Fowler,"

"Yes, sir?"

"The young woman, Agent Vane; she acquitted herself well?"

"Absolutely. She is a thorough professional."

The Director was silent for a moment. "Very good. I'll wait for your report —and hers." He sat at his desk and picked up a file.

Dismissed.

(29)

The paperwork and red tape irritated Fowler and Kendall. The wait while the paper pushers at the DOJ dotted Is and crossed Ts was infuriating, but the Director wanted to be sure that Marcoletto didn't slip away because some slick lawyer spotted a chink in their legal armor.

The afternoon segued into evening, and Fowler, sent out for sandwiches. He, Kendall, and Sally sat in his office going over details of the operation.

"Surveilance teams are watching the front and back of both buildings," Kendall told Sally. "They'll see who comes and goes."

"And you're sure the two buildings are connected," Sally said.

Fowler set down his coffee.

"The Mainline Storage warehouse is titled to one of Marcoletto's men. When we were in the Blue Bunny, we saw a window up the wall between the club and the warehouse. I'm betting that's Marcoletto's hangout."

"We have to get a handle on both buildings at once in case people escape from one to the other."

There was silence for a minute, and Sally said, "This waiting is awful. Do you ever get used to it?"

"Never," Fowler said. "It's the worst part of the job. Except for the paper-work."

Doctor Evan Burns had just finished his supper and had settled into his easy chair with his newspaper and his evening glass of scotch over ice. In the kitchen, his wife Ruth was at the sink washing the supper dishes. She was humming, happy with the chore.

It was a good life, His medical practice wasn't the most prestigious in the city; he didn't treat the Congressmen or cabinet members, but he made a comfortable living taking care of the government workers, business professionals, and their families. And unlike the doctors who treated the government bigwigs, he wasn't on call at a moment's notice. His evenings and weekends were his own; all in all, a good trade.

He was turning to the sports page when Ruth's humming stopped. "Evan?" she said, her voice quavering. He'd heard that voice before, when she'd seen a spider scuttling across the floor, or a centipede crawling out of the drain.

Burns set down his drink and took his glasses off his nose. He started down the hallway, rolling up the newspaper to swat whatever had invaded the kitchen. "What is it, honey?"

He stepped through the doorway and found a grinning man in a sharkskin suit slouched against the sink, a carving knife held loosely in his fingers. In the corner, a hulking brute strained the shoulders of his sport coat, one hand over Ruth's mouth, the other groping her breast. Her eyes were wild with terror over Tuds' thick fingers.

"Evening, Doc," Shimmy said.

"What —who are you? Take your hands off my wife!" He started toward her and Shimmy stepped between them, twirling the knife in his fingers to grip the handle, blade up.

"Easy, Doc." He slipped the point of the knife into the placket of Ruth's dress, just under her chin. His hand twitched, and a white pearl button clicked on the linoleum. "Your wife's real pretty." Another button. "I'd hate to see anything bad happen to her just because you can't hold your water."

"Who are you? What do you want?" The words tumbled out. "Money? I don't have a lot here, but you can have it. My wife's jewelry —anything. Just don't hurt her."

Another button. "We don't want your money, Doc, in fact you'll be paid real good. We got a sick friend needs attention. All you got to do is what you do every day. The sooner you come along, the sooner you and wife here can get back to domestic bliss."

Another button. The placket of the dress was sagging, and Burns could see the lace of Ruth's slip.

"How about it, Doc? I'm running out of buttons."

"All right." He heaved a sigh. "All right. I'll cooperate. But she comes with me. I'm not leaving her with him."

"Sure, Doc. She can come too. Got your bag here, or is it in the car?"

"In the hall closet. And you," he pointed a finger at Tuds. "Take your paw off my wife's breast."

Tuds looked to Shimmy, who nodded. "Treat the lady with respect, Tuds. Doc's on the team now. Right, Doc?"

"I, I —Yes." I have to do this, he thought. It's the only chance we'll come out of this alive.

In five minutes, Burns was in the front seat beside Shimmy, and Ruth was in the back seat with Tuds. Take a look in the back, Doc," Shimmy said, "just in case you get any ideas."

Burns turned his head to see Ruth, weeping silently. Tuds had an arm around her, one huge hand locked on her shoulder, the other clamped on her larynx.

Burns turned back and stared through the windshield, saying nothing for the rest of the ride.

Shimmy gave the signal and the warehouse door rolled up. He pulled the car inside, and in the dim light, Burns saw stacks of crates. Shimmy shut off the engine. "Here we are, Doc." He stepped out of the car and said, "C'mon." He jerked his head. "Your missus can stay in the car with Tuds for the moment."

The doctor turned to his wife and looked into her wide, staring eyes. "It'll be all right, Ruth. I promise." Clutching his bag, Burns stepped out into the warehouse.

"Right this way, Doc." Shimmy grinned that crooked grin of his, and Burns wanted to slap it off his face. He followed Shimmy to a tower built into a corner of the warehouse. The mobster rapped on the door and it swung open.

The ground floor room looked like the card room at his golf club, sofas, armchairs, a wet bar. The difference was the rack of firearms near the stairs leading to the second floor. Burns was in the War. He was a Medic, but they still taught him how to shoot in basic training. If he had a chance, he'd take it, but he had Ruth to consider.

On a leather sofa against the wall, a man lay, his shirt open and his head pillowed by his suit jacket. His mouth was slack, and a silvery string of drool hung from its corner to pool on the couch.

The patient, for that's how Burns saw him, looked strange. His face drooped, forming wattles of flesh that folded over each other.

He'd seen the look before on a patient who was obese until he developed cancer and wasted away, leaving his skin hanging loose like an oversized sweater.

The man was feverish, sweating. Burns reached into his bag and pulled out a thermometer. "What's his name?"

"No names, Doc."

"I need to talk to him. I can't just call him 'Hey You.'"

"Call him Tommy."

Burns slapped Pouch's cheek gently. "Tommy." No response. "Tommy!" He slapped a little harder. The eyes opened, out of focus.

"Uh, what —who?"

"I'm Doctor Burns, Tommy. I'm here to make you better." He shook down the mercury in the thermometer and put it between Pouch's lips. "Hold it under your tongue, and don't bite down on it."

Burns pulled out his stethoscope and listened to Pouch's heart. He timed it with the second hand of his wrist watch. The pulse was rapid and a little weak. Through the open shirt Burns saw patches of gauze taped to the patient's torso.

He peeled back the tape on one and Pouch winced. Under the gauze was a neat row of sutures, some of them oozing greenish-yellow pus. He also saw lily white scars from old incisions all over the abdomen. Burns palpated the area and felt something hard and flat under the dermis. Rectangular, with sharp corners. The patient jerked when Burns touched a tender spot.

The skin was hot to the touch and an angry red. The man had an infection, no doubt of it. The first tiny bloodspots were already appearing on the skin.

He pulled out the thermometer and read it. "This man is suffering from septicemia, blood poisoning. He needs to be in a hospital."

"Well, like you might've guessed, pal, that ain't in the cards. You take care of him, here and now."

"I'll need medication for him."

Burns weighed the situation. He pulled out his prescription pad and scribbled the needed drugs on it. He tore the page off the pad and handed it to Shimmy. "These."

Shimmy studied the prescription. "Yeah, I think we can manage this."

"What's sewn up inside him?"

Shimmy's grin went flat. "You know what they say about cats and curiosity? Works for people, too. And their wives. Just fix him up, Doc. Just fix him up."

Across the room, Tuds half carried Ruth through the door. He pushed her onto another sofa and sat beside her, draping an arm across her shoulders. Ruth seemed to be shrinking into herself, her lip quivering, and her blue eyes tearing.

I'll get you out of this, honey, Burns thought. Whatever it takes.

(30)

Twenty-two agents crowded the briefing room. The D.C. office was devoting all its resources to the strike, and Fowler was making the most of it.

"We have surveillance on the warehouse and the Blue Bunny, and we're waiting for confirmation that Marcoletto is on the premises," Fowler said. "We believe the two buildings are connected, possibly with a tunnel or hidden corridor backstage. Because of this, we will hit both buildings simultaneously."

Kendall pointed to a diagram on an easel. "Based on the blueprints filed with the zoning Office, the main entrance to the warehouse is a twenty-by-fourteen lift door. A pedestrian door is eight feet to the right. No windows in the front, two at street level in the rear. A single door opens onto the alley behind, thirty-two feet from the stage door of the Blue Bunny. One team will enter the warehouse and another the nightclub at the same time. That means four of agents on the street and four in the alley to cover any potential escape."

"That seems a little lean. No backup from D.C. Metro?" one of the agents asked.

Fowler shook his head.

"How about Treasury? Isn't this case in their bailliwick?"

"No dice. This operation is strictly in-house. Director's orders."

Kendall continued. "According to the blueprints, the Mainline Storage warehouse is just a big brick box. We have no way of knowing what may be inside, or what changes may have been made to the building. Be prepared for surprises."

"The Blue Bunny is a different story. Agent Kendall and I have been inside recently and have had a look at the place."

"I bet that's not all you got a look at," a voice came from the back of the room. There were snickers, and Sally rolled her eyes.

"Knock it off!" Fowler snapped. "These are dangerous people. Marcoletto's got muscle in there. Even the maitre d' is carrying. Marcoletto's got two gorillas on the sidewalk and at least eight men inside counting the stage hands. The Bunny is no cakewalk."

Kendall put another diagram on the easel, this one showing the layout of the nightclub. "The building is linear; entrance, foyer, show floor, stage, dressing rooms. Watch out for the curtained portals on either side of the stage. We saw men come out of both, and the curtains provide cover for shooters. Study the floor plan so you can find your way around if we have to use tear gas."

"The problem we have in the Bunny is the civilian clientele," Fowler said, "so no shotguns. We want to shoot bad guys only."

"How do we tell them apart?"

"Bad guys have guns," Kendall said. "good guys don't. Rule of thumb: bad guys are on their feet, good guys are sitting at the tables drooling. My advice is aim high and watch out for the waitresses."

"We are looking particularly for these men," Fowler said, as Kendall put a poster board on the easel. Taped to it were enlargements of Stroud's BEP photo, an old mug shot of Marcoletto, and a sketch artist's rendering of Pouch drawn from Betty's description.

"The man in the middle is probably recognizable to most of you, Mob boss Tito Marcoletto. The man to the left is James Stroud, suspect in the BEP heist. The man on the right –"

"Looks like my aunt's Shar Pei."

Laughter broke out but was immediately stifled by a hard look from Fowler. "The man to the right we know only by a nickname, Pouch."

"We want these guys," Kendall said, "alive if possible."

"Marcoletto is a big catch, but this one –" Fowler tapped Pouch's picture with his forefinger. "He's the prize in the Cracker Jack.

"I'll lead the team into the Mainline warehouse, Agent Kendall's going to lead at the Bunny. Agent Vane will go on that team to oversee the, uh, female employees.

"Four men outside," he went on, "front and back, eight with me, eight with Agent Kendall. We'll all wear vests."

An agent in the back of the room raised his hand. "With all due respect, Agent Fowler, if this warehouse is Marcoletto's headquarters, we can't just knock on the door. How will we breach the entrance?"

For the first time in the briefing, Fowler smiled. "I have that covered."

As the group broke out into their teams, Sally hung back for a moment. She was wearing a black turtleneck sweater and tailored trousers. A pair of steel-toed oxfords completed the outfit. Her hair was wound in a tight bun.

"You look like a dangerous version of Katherine Hepburn."

Her mouth twitched up at one corner. "Thanks, I think. On one hand, I wish I was on your team, on the other hand, I see why it's not a good idea."

"We'd both be watching each other with one eye. We can't afford the distraction."

"I agree. I get it, but that doesn't make it any easier."

"For me either. It's the life. Better get with your team."

"I want to give you a kiss for luck, Dan, but then everybody'd want one. This will have to do." Sally kissed the tip of her forefinger and touched it to his lips.

"There'll be plenty of kisses later, Sally. I promise."

"That's one you better keep, Buster."

Fowler and Kendall were instructing their teams when the door opened and a clerk came in with a sheaf of papers. He handed them to Fowler, who leafed through them, ticking them off in his head. "Gentlemen," he looked over to Sally, "and lady, "the warrants are live. The operation is a go."

It had been three hours since Shimmy and Tuds had brought Doctor Burns to Marcoletto's headquarters. They couldn't get Prontisil, but they brought plenty of penicillin. Burns shot Pouch up with a double dose, and the fever was coming down slowly. In an hour, he'd give him another injection. It would give him major stomach issues, but at this moment, it was a small consideration.

His orders were to get "Tommy" on his feet and lucid as quickly as possible. The sooner he did, the sooner he could get out of there and take Ruth with him. If, and it was a big if, the animals didn't kill them both. Tommy had mumbled enough in his delirium to tell Burns what was going on. He'd said "plates" more than once. Based on the size and shape of the incisions and the implants, what kind of plates was obvious.

The big guy, Tuds the little one called him, sat on a sofa across the room. He didn't have a hand on Ruth, but he was hip to hip against her, his shoulder hemming her into the upholstered wraparound corner.

Ruth had stopped weeping. She'd cried herself out a long time ago. She sat and stared at nothing, probably in shock.

One of the medicines Burns requested was morphine. When Shimmy stepped away to mix himself a drink, Burns filled two syringes with the pain killer and set them on the table beside his stethescope.

They watched him close early on, but the longer he was there, the less diligent they became, thinking Burns was fearful enough for his wife's safety to make no trouble. He reached into the bag and opened the leather case that held a pair of scalpels. He quickly slid one up the sleeve of his shirt, tucking it under the leather strap of his watch. There were four of them in the room, Tuds, the little guy Shimmy, one they called Pug, and a young guy named Jimmy who looked as nervous to be there as Burns himself.

Burns had kept his eyes open and saw where each of them carried his gun. If he could disable any one of them, just long enough to grab one, he and Ruth might have a chance. The guns in the rack would be better, but Pug sat in a chair, blocking the way.

Wait, watch, be ready, he told himself. If there's a chance, it will come only once.

The team was ready; everyone suited up, equipment loaded, and cars lined up in the motor pool garage. The agents gathered around Fowler for final instructions.

"We may run into anything inside," he told the team. "Follow procedure. Everything by the book. Watch out for civilians, and above all, watch each other's backs. We want this quick and clean. Any last questions?"

There was a moment's silence, and Fowler said, "Time to roll." He and Sally shared a final glance, and he climbed into the passenger seat of the Rammer.

The convoy rolled out of the garage and turned south.

Across the street, Plug Sandrock sat in an unmarked car. As soon as he saw the Rammer, he keyed the radio.

"This is Detective Sandrock. Give me the Duty Officer."

Tito pulled the drape aside and looked down on the floor of the Bunny. A better crowd than usual for a Wednesday. A gang of GIs on leave filled four tables, and horny men in twos and threes occupied all the others but three. One table caught his attention, two guys in suits. Each had a drink in front of him, untouched. Each had his hat on the table, a hand beside it.

Tito pulled binoculars from a desk drawer and took another look. Their backs were turned to him, but the one on the right had Fed stitched all over him.

Tito punched the intercom. "Pug, tell Slick to buzz upstairs." Maybe I worry too much, Marcoletto thought, but maybe I don't worry enough.

"Yeah, Boss?" It was Slick.

"The two suits at the front table. When did they arrive?"

"Maybe an hour or so. They tipped me good for a primo spot."

"They're clean?"

"Looked that way. I didn't spot any sign of a piece on either one. I put a hand on the back of both of them to steer them to the table. No shoulder rigs."

Tito thought a moment. Tell Bimbo and Pic to get close. I think those two have badges, and I have a good idea what's under the hats.

"Will do."

Tito buzzed Pug again. "What's the doc say? How's our boy?"

There was silence for a few seconds then Pug came back on. "Doc says his fever's down. He's awake but he ain't sittin' up."

Tito snapped off the intercom. At least that much was going the right direction. The question is, he thought, what do I do with the doctor and his wife? Maybe I can get him to work for me, replace the rummy, but will his woman keep her trap shut? Not likely. In the big picture, they both are expendable.

His supper sat untouched on his desk. Who could eat in the middle of this?

If things went right, Pouch could still walk up the gangplank of the Bella Maria on the twenty-third under his own steam, and once he was past the three-mile limit, he'd be out of the Feds' reach. There'd be a reception committee for him at the dock in Livorno, and once Mussolini's people had him, extradition wasn't even a consideration.

Treasury Agent Barney Short was enjoying the show, but Ennis Cooper was uncomfortable. He wanted nothing to do with the Blue Bunny and the degenerates in it, but after Fowler's mention of Tito Marcoletto, Cooper felt compelled to explore the lead on his own. Enquiry led him to this den of depravity.

The dark-haired stripper on the runway was down to a G-string, and the hooting, sweating patrons around them were eating it up.

She wiggled her torso and the crowd roared. She turned her back and hooked her thumbs in the G-string, tugging it down, inch by tantalizing inch, left side, right side, while the band played a sultry slow burner.

Short whistled between his fingers and when he saw Cooper's disapproving look, he shrugged. "Hey, we're undercover. Have to fit in. Loosen up."

The waitress came to their table. She looked at their untouched drinks and said, "So, gents, what'll it be? Two more of the same?"

Cooper turned his head and found himself staring at the server's bust. Raising his voice to be heard over the raucous music and the raucous crowd, he averted his eyes and said, "We haven't finished these yet."

"Two drink minimum, honey," she said. "Now or later."

"Come back in a little while," Short said with a leer. "And bring a friend with you."

Distracted by the waitress, neither Cooper nor Short noticed the hulking bouncers coming up behind them. One of them nodded to the other and they grabbed Short's and Cooper's jackets by the lapels and yanked them down to their elbows, pinning their arms.

Bimbo lifted Cooper out of his chair like a doll and held him on his toes so he couldn't break away and run. He said in Cooper's ear. "Come quiet."

The bouncers frog marched Cooper and Short backstage and shoved them into an unoccupied dressing room.

"What's the meaning of this?" Cooper sputtered. "We were just watching the show."

Bimbo put a finger to his lips. "Shhhh. Boss says take you backstage, I don't argue." The waitress brought their hats and handed them to Bimbo. "Thanks, doll." He reached into Cooper's and pulled out a blue-steel .32 automatic.

"Just watchin' the show, huh?"

Cooper and Short shared a look.

"The Boss don't like people packin' in his club. Who you planning to shoot? Fat Jack? Don't like his jokes?"

"Nobody," Cooper said, trying to keep his voice even. "I carry that for protection."

Bimbo turned Short's hat over and found a small revolver in the lining. "And what's your excuse?"

No reply from Short.

"Have a seat," Bimbo said, shoving Cooper into a chair. "Boss'll get to you when he does." Pic set Short in another chair. Bimbo took sashes from some kimonos hanging on the rack and tied the agents to their chairs.

"Watch 'em, Pic. I'll go call upstairs."

Bimbo left. Pic set a chair in front of the agents and the door and dropped his bulk in it. He folded his arms, a pistol in one meaty paw, and gave them the blank stare of the purposefully stupid.

(31)

Tito pressed a panel to the left of his desk, and a section of the wall swung inward. The secret exit gave onto a flight of stairs that opened below, backstage at the Bunny.

Downstairs, he found Cooper and Short sitting in chairs, under Pic's watchful eye. Tito smiled affably. "So what do we have here, Pic?"

"These two were packin' heat, Boss."

"Look," Cooper blurted, this is all just a misunderstanding. We –"

Tito's smile flattened. "Shut it. You come in here totin' guns. I bet you're both totin' badges too. Am I right?" He turned to Bimbo. "Empty their pockets."

Bimbo rifled the agents' pockets and piled the contents on a dressing table. Tito picked up a brown leather foldover. He flipped it open and saw the badge and the I.D. His eyebrows rose. "Treasury Department." He opened the other one and found the same thing. You're Cooper, you're Short, or do I have it backwards?"

He pulled a chair and straddled it, arms over the top. "So tell me. I'm all ears. What are two Feds doing in my night club?"

"We just came for the show," Short said. "Honest."

"You and that librarian?" Tito jerked his head at Cooper. "Don't make me laugh. Time to start talking, boys." His smile returned. "We've got all night."

Two streets over from the Bunny, Fowler and Kendall were waiting for the go ahead from their surveillance team. The spies had seen Tito enter the warehouse hours before, and so far, they hadn't seen him leave it.

The raid was scheduled for 11:05. Fowler climbed into the passenger seat of the Rammer. "Two minutes to Showtime, Barney." The agent behind the wheel nodded and smiled grimly. From the corner of his eye Fowler saw Barney cross himself.

Swooping in on wheels, Fowler usually stood on the running board, pistol in hand, but when the battering ram smashed the warehouse doors, he didn't want to smack his face on the door frame or the wreckage.

The car behind them flashed its lights.

Ready.

Tito was back in his office. The Treasury boys weren't talking —yet, but before the night was over, they'd tell him more than he ever wanted to know. He would have had Bimbo take them to a pasture somewhere and ice them, but first, he needed to know what the Feds knew, and those glorified bookkeepers were going to tell him.

He looked at the cold meal on his desk. A T-bone steak, a baked potato, and beans. He was suddenly hungry. He picked up the steak in his hand and gnawed a bite out of it. Even cold it tasted better than he expected. Two more days and Pouch will be on his way to the Old country, Tito thought, and I'll be on my way to the top.

He took another bite out of the steak and chased it with a swallow of scotch. The drink needed freshened. He buzzed downstairs. "Pug, bring me another scotch."

"Okay, boss."

Maybe Marcoletto was worrying too much, but he didn't think so. The Plan was a Make or Break proposition, and he was going to push every inch to Make.

Pug brought Tito his drink and was halfway down the stairs when all hell broke loose.

A lot happened at once.

The Rammer rumbled down the street.

"It's going to be tough to get a good angle on the door with the street parked up on both sides," Barney said.

"Do what you have to," Fowler said.

"Yes, sir."

They passed under the blue glow of the Bunny sign and saw Kendall and the agents approaching the bouncers from both directions.

One of the bouncers saw the steel wedge on the Rammer and grabbed his partner's coat sleeve, but before they could sound a warning inside the club, they had other things to deal with.

Kendall and his men were running, their badges and guns out. "Federal agents! Freeze!"

One did; one didn't. One put his hands up; one put his hand into his coat. Both fell in a hail of bullets.

Barney swung the truck as wide as he could, clipping a few parked cars as he did, and hit the roll up door to the warehouse at an oblique angle. The steel reinforced door buckled but didn't come off its tracks.

"Dammit!" Barney shouted. He threw the truck into reverse and floored the gas pedal. The Rammer lurched backward across the street to back into a Packard convertible and shoved it sideways over the sidewalk and into the building beside it.

Barney floored it again. He had a straight shot this time and the impact ripped the door from its tracks with a screech of tearing metal and shoved it to the side. The truck smashed through the sham crates and a Bureau sedan behind pulled in at an angle, blocking the entrance.

Fowler swung the passenger door open and stepped out, using it as a shield. "FBI! Come out with your hands up."

His words were met with bullets. Shots whanged off the door and roof of the truck. Fowler and his men returned the fire, and the gunmen retreated behind the concrete tower.

"Barney!" Fowler shouted, "Ram the tower!"

He looked into the cab and saw Barney slumped over the wheel. He pulled Barney out the passenger side and one of the agents dragged him to safety.

Fowler slid behind the wheel and jerked the gearshift into low. The Rammer splintered the stacks of crates like match wood and brought its wedge to bear on the tower entrance.

The door buckled, taking a lot of the concrete with it. The broken concrete around the door gave Fowler an Idea. The truck rumbled forward again, and he aimed the wedge to the right of the broken doorway.

Like a chisel on stone, the wedge took out a chunk of the wall. Fowler was about to back up for a third pass when he saw people inside, five men and a woman.

The sound of gunfire on the sidewalk was drowned out by the band inside the Bunny. The agents swarmed through the doors and Slick reached for the button under his podium to sound the alarm. Before he could, two agents grabbed him and threw him to the carpet.

They burst onto the show floor and almost no one noticed until Kendall fired a shot at the ceiling. "FBI! Nobody move!" The band stopped in mid measure and the patrons froze for a second then as if on a signal, all leapt from their chairs and ran for the front, bowling over Kendall and his team in a mad scramble for the exit.

Cooper and Short heard three things: sudden silence as the music stopped, gunfire, and pounding on the door.

"Pic!" a voice shouted, "Trouble out front!"

The bouncer pulled an automatic from his waistband and left, locking the door behind him.

"Now what?" Short said.

"I have no idea," Cooper snapped. "If you have any suggestions, let me know."

The patrons surged through the foyer, only to find an ugly green Pontiac blocking the doors. Some followed the musicians through the curtains to the dressing rooms and out the alley door only to find themselves staring down the barrels of the agents' weapons.

Shots from the bar. Bimbo, Pic, and the bartenders were hunkered down, firing shotguns and pistols. Kendall caught a bullet in the shoulder that spun him halfway around, and Sally, standing beside him, fired a three shot triangle that put the shooter on the floor.

Kendall looked down and saw the slug caught in his vest. "Lucky me," he muttered, and went back to firing.

One of the agents opened up with a Tommy gun, spraying the bar with shards of mirrors, glasses, and bottles. Tito's men, realizing they were getting the worst of it, threw their guns onto the bar.

"Don't shoot!" Bimbo shouted. "We quit!"

Pug's first instinct was to protect his boss. He grabbed a Thompson from the gun rack and dashed up the stairs.

"Don't shoot!" Bimbo shouted. "We quit!"

Doctor Burns was bent over Pouch when the Rammer broke down the door. Shimmy ran across the room and grabbed the other Thompson from the rack. Tuds pulled his automatic and tugged Ruth in front of him as a shield.

The Rammer slammed the wall, breaking a double doorway in the concrete. Shimmy flipped the poker table on edge and fired a spray of bullets from behind it. Lead bounced off the wedge on the front of the rammer and blew out the windshield.

Fowler rolled out of the driver's door and took cover behind Marcoletto's sedan as .50 caliber rounds peppered the truck.

Tito heard the muffled shots too, and before he could raise Pug on the intercom, a crash shook the building. More gunfire. Louder. What the hell was going on?

Then it hit him. Pouch was downstairs. Tito had to see that he was safe. Everything was riding on him getting on that boat.

Tito opened the top drawer of his desk and pulled out a .45 automatic. He was out the door of his office and about to start down the stairs when Pug came running up, a machine gun in his hands.

"Get back inside, Boss. It's Feds raiding."

"Pouch. Is he all right?"

"He's still downstairs with the doc."

"Get him!" Tito shouted. "Bring him up here! Now!"

Pug scrambled down the stairs. The tower shook as the Rammer hit for the second time. Pug couldn't hold the gun and drag Pouch up the stairs at the same time.

He propped the machine gun against the wall halfway down the stairs and ran for the sofa where Pouch was sitting up with the doc beside him. He shouted at Stroud, "Help me lift him. We have to get him upstairs. Stroud locked his arms under Pouch's armpits and dragged him backwards toward the stairs. Pug took his feet.

At the top, Tito stood in the office door, gun in hand. When Pug reached the top, Stroud dragged Pouch inside and Pug retrieved his gun. He ran into Tito's office and saw Stroud and the boss pulling Pouch into the secret exit.

Carrying Ruth in front of him, Tuds fired around her shoulder as he moved for the stairs. Fowler's team hung back because of the heavy fire and fear of hitting the woman.

One of the agents jumped into the bed of the Rammer and fired a volley of shots over the cab. He hit Shimmy in the chest three times, and the thug went over backwards, the Thompson spraying the ceiling.

Fowler shifted position, angling for a clear shot at Tuds without hitting his hostage.

It wasnt necessary.

A ricochet nicked Tuds' ear, and that was all the distraction Burns needed.

"Bastard!" The doctor leapt from the sofa, hypodermic needles in both hands, thumbs on the plungers. He drove the needles into either side of Tuds' thick neck and emptied them.

Tuds grunted in pain. His mouth moved but nothing came out. His eyes rolled back in his head and he let go of Ruth, who fell forward, leaving Tuds without a shield. He raised his pistol with a wavering hand and fired aimlessly.

Fowler put a slug between the mobster's eyes, and. the back of Tuds' skull exploded in a gory spray.

(32)

Upstairs, Pug broke the glass of the warehouse window. He fired down on the warehouse floor with the Thompson, hitting one agent and sending another scrambling for cover.

He was safe for the moment. The office door was the same as the one downstairs and the sons of bitches sure as hell weren't driving that truck up the stairs.

Fowler and his men climbed over the truck and the rubble to find Burns holding his wife. Both were weeping. "Get them out of here," he told one of his men, and started for the stairs.

"Got a shooter upstairs with a Tommy gun!" one of the agents shouted through the doorway. "He got Williams."

"Masks on! Gas him!"

An agent pulled on his mask and raised a short-barreled rifle to his shoulder and fired. The tear gas cartridge went through the warehouse window and began filling the office with choking blue-white fumes.

Pug ran to the emergency exit and frantically tugged at the panel. It wouldn't open. Tito had locked it when he got on the other side.

A second cartridge went through the warehouse window, bounced off the ceiling, and added to the lung–burning smoke that filled the office. Pug's eyes teared up and his chest heaved. He had to get out of that room.

Fowler climbed the stairs quietly with two men behind him, a riot gun aimed at the door on the landing. The shooting from above had stopped. He could hear no sound from inside over the noise from elsewhere.

He signaled Dennison, the man behind him and the agent moved to the other side of the stairwell. One step. Another step.

The steel door swung wide, banging against the wall. Pug burst into the hallway, choking and coughing. Before he could bring his gun to bear, double-aught buckshot knocked him backward. He bounced off the wall, dropped his gun, then fell forward to roll down the stairwell. Fowler clambered over Pug's body and up the stairs with his men behind him.

Fowler jacked another round and swung the riot gun ahead of him around the doorframe. The office was empty. The tear gas was thick in Tito's office and Fowler was glad for his mask.

He pulled the drape aside and looked down into the Bunny. Kendall's team had customers, musicians, and the waitresses corralled in the orchestra pit. But where was Marcoletto? And where was the courier, the one Betty called Pouch?

The office looked wrong. No closets, but the width was short a good two feet. "Break through the walls." Fowler's voice was muffled by the mask. He attacked the wall with the butt of his shotgun, sending lath and plaster flying.

"Here!" an agent called. Through a hole he'd made, Fowler saw stairs leading downward. He kicked his way through the plaster at the bottom and squeezed between the joists. "Come on!" He shouted over his shoulder and started down the steps to the Bunny.

Below, Tito and Stroud had Pouch by the armpits, his feet dragging on the floor. People were running in every direction as if the place were on fire, and the trio had to fight the surge of bodies to go in the opposite direction. A brunette in a flowered kimono bounced off Tito as she ran.

"This way!" he shouted, steering Stroud to the left. They came to a broom closet and Tito yanked open the door. He kicked mops and buckets out of the way and threw his shoulder against the back wall. It opened a narrow stairwell leading downward into darkness. Tito flicked his lighter and led the way, walking crabwise to guide Pouch down the narrow steps.

The stairway opened into a tunnel under the Bunny. If he could get Pouch away, he could spirit him aboard the Bella Maria and sail with him, get out of the country. The dons in Sicily would welcome them both with open arms. All he had to do was get out of D.C.

Stroud stumbled on the stairs and pitched forward into Pouch and Tito. Tito dropped his lighter and the tunnel went dark. All three rolled down the stairs and landed in a heap on the packed earth floor.

Tito cursed. Pouch cried out in pain.

"I can't find my lighter," Tito snarled, patting the floor.

"I have mine." Stroud said. In a second, flickering light filled the passage.

Pouch lay on his back, clutching his stomach. Tito pulled Pouch's hand away and saw a spreading blotch of red on the courier's shirt.

"Goddammit! He's bleeding. Help me get him up."

Stroud hauled Pouch to his feet, and the courier groaned.

"It's only half a block," Marcoletto snarled. "Come on."

Stroud had his arms around Pouch's waist and the blood was making him slippery. "I can't hold onto him."

Marcoletto whirled around and put the muzzle of his pistol an inch from Stroud's eye. "You drop him, I'll drop you. Now move!"

The tunnel led under the street where a sidewalk elevator was waiting. Tito threw the switch and overhead, the flaps opened as the platform rose.

Fowler and his men went from room to room backstage kicking in doors and sending strippers screaming into the chaos in the hallways. He couldn't let Marcoletto get away with Pouch and the plates.

"Agent Fowler!" Dennison said, "There's a door that isn't on the floor plan! Over there!"

Two customers made it to the street somehow, and piled into their car, but before they could escape, the driver's door was yanked open and he was pulled out and thrown into the street. "Hey! What the hell –"

Tito shot him in the head. The man in the passenger seat jumped out and ran.

"Come on!" Tito shouted at Stroud who was dragging Pouch from the sidewalk elevator. "Get him in the car."

Stroud had the back door open and was pushing Pouch into the car. "Tito –" Stroud was staring back the way he'd come. The elevator was going back down.

Marcoletto stepped on the starter and the engine growled into life. Stroud jumped in and Tito threw the car in gear. As he did, flashing lights and sirens swept into the block from both ends.

D.C Metro had joined the party with Plug Sandrock in the lead.

Both ends of the streets were blocked with squad cars. Through the windshield, Tito saw the elevator again at street level and standing beside it, Dan Fowler.

The mobster roared in rage and threw the car in gear, aiming it for the agent. Fowler raised his gun and fired three rapid shots through the windshield. He threw down the riot gun and drew his automatic.

The sedan veered onto the sidewalk and crashed into the wall of a warehouse. Tito staggered out, blood streaming down his face, pistol in his fist.

"Drop it, Marcoletto. It's over."

"The hell it is!"

Tito fired two shots before Fowler fired one that caught him in the chest. The gangster pitched forward onto his knees and his gun clattered onto the pavement.

Pouch half fell out of the car and staggered to Tito's side. Nobody was going to take him alive. He scooped up the gun, and Fowler fired, hitting him in the left side of his gut. Pouch screamed and fell beside Tito.

When Tito saw where Pouch was hit, he wept.

(33)

In the club, resistance died quickly.

The panicked patrons and waitresses who tried to run out the front doors of the Bunny found the entrance blocked and bounced off each other in a confused mass.

"Keep them in the foyer til we can sort them out," Kendall told one of the agents. He turned to go back to the show floor and a man in a suit got his attention.

"Sir! Sir!" he said, waving his arms. "Are you in charge here?"

"Maybe," Kendall said, "Why?"

He lowered his voice. "My name is Hainesford. I'm an aide to Congressman Hesse. That's him in the corner with his hat brim pulled down."

An older man cowered in a nook behind Slick's podium. He had his forearm over the lower part of his face, and his eyes darted around like a cornered rabbit's.

"I'd appreciate it if you'd let me get him out of here before he's, you know, recognized."

"I have an operation in progress here, Haines." Kendall turned away, and the aide grabbed his arm.

"Now you listen –" Haines' order was cut short by a left hook that sent him reeling back into the gaggle of customers and waitresses.

"Cuff them together, Mac," Kendall said. He shot a look at Hesse. "All of them."

Back inside, the agents had customers, staff, and the few of Tito's men still standing gathered at gunpoint in the orchestra pit.

"We aren't arresting all these people, are we?" Sally asked.

Kendall shook his head. "No, not all, but we won't tell them yet."

"Agent Kendall." It was Frost, whose bulk barely fit in his vest. "I have a situation I'm not sure about. Could you come with me?"

Backstage, Frost led Fowler to a dressing room where he found two men in suits tied to chairs.

"Untie us!" The one in the rimless glasses said, petulance in his voice. "We're Federal agents!"

"Their credentials are over there." Frost pointed to the pile of their belongings on the vanity table.

Kendall picked up the foldovers and read each one. He smiled. "This is highly irregular, gentlemen. I'm not in charge of this operation. I'll have to consult Agent Fowler as to official protocol. He's running the show. He's a little busy right now, but he'll get to you eventually. In the meantime, sit tight." Kendall walked out on the sputtering Cooper and barely made it three steps before he burst out laughing.

On the street the D.C. patrolmen swarmed around the entrance to the Bunny. Plug sauntered over to Fowler, who stood beside Marcoletto and Plug.

"Welcome to the party, Plug. This guy didn't kill your floater." He nudged Tito with the toe of his shoe. "But odds are good you can nail him for conspiracy. But you'll have to wait in line. The Attorney General has first dibs."

"I hope you got the paper for this rodeo, Fowler. Who do you think you are, pullin' this stunt without notifying Metro?"

"Orders, Plug."

"From who?" Plug sneered, "your evil little dwarf of a Director?"

"Better yet, Plug, the man in the wheelchair."

Plug's face went blank.

"You know the guy," Fowler went on. "Lives in a big white house on Pennsylvania Avenue?" He let this sink in, and even in the Blue light from the argon rabbit, he could see Sandrock's face flush.

"Good thing you boys are slow, Plug. A few minutes earlier, and you would have bollixed the whole thing. We're talking National Security here. Now, if you really want to be helpful, get on the radio and call us some ambulances."

Fowler looked down at the crooks on the pavement. "I'd like these two to live long enough to be convicted. And while you're at it, Plug, send a paddy wagon. We'll have people to transport."

Four hours later, it was over. The paddy wagon took the living, and the meat wagon took the dead. Fowler, Kendall, and Sally sat in the bed of the Rammer, legs dangling over the edge as agents chained the doors of the Bunny shut.

Marcoletto and Pouch were in the Police ward of D.C. General Hospital, and both were expected to live. Stroud was in a holding cell at headquarters, and the bulk of the crowd rounded up in the raid were guests for the night at D.C. Metro's Central Station.

"Marcoletto's finished," Kendall said. "Stroud's singing like Caruso. He can't talk fast enough."

"Don't count Marcoletto out yet," Fowler said. "I got a look at the files in those two cabinets in his office. He's got dirt on enough high,-stepping people to pardon John Wilkes Booth."

"But we've got the files now, right, Dan?" Sally said.

"They're on their way to headquarters. I imagine there'll be a lot of nervous politicians tomorrow morning."

"They'll be destroyed, won't they?"

"Not right away. They're material evidence if the Attorney General decides to prosecute Marcoletto on blackmail charges, Sally."

"Did Marcoletto really think this plot would endear the Mob to Mussolini?"

"The pipe dream of the century," Fowler said.

""Tito rolled a jumbo set of dice," said Kendall. "And he crapped out."

"If everything I've read about Il Duce is true, he'd double-cross his own mother. He would have taken the plates and ignored the source. Tito would have come up empty. His ambition was doomed from the start."

"I think this occasion calls for a drink," Larry said.

Sally laughed. "Don't tell me you brought a flask on a raid."

"Nope. Even better. Kendall reached behind him and brought out a bottle of Seven Stars champagne. "Found this behind the bar. Anybody have a cork-screw?"

"Nope," Fowler said.

Sally shook her head.

Kendall shrugged and broke off the neck against the side of the truck. Foam erupted from the bottle, and when it died down, Kendall raised it in salute and took a long drink. He offered the bottle to Dan and Sally.

"Watch your lips on the edge."

"I've got better things to do with my lips," Sally said, and pulled Dan's face to hers.

Larry shrugged and raised the bottle again. "I'll drink to that."

(34)

Fowler picked up his customary newspapers a few hours later. There was no mention of the raid in any of them. It happened too late at night, but it would be all over the afternoon editions.

He'd had no time to sleep, but he did enjoy a shower, a shave and a quick breakfast before heading to the office.

A box was waiting on his desk. He opened it and found a small bundle wrapped in a hospital towel. He tucked it under his arm and headed for the Director's office.

The Director's secretary looked up as he approached and waved him on. "You're expected, Agent Fowler. Please go in."

The first thing Fowler noticed when he entered the Director's office was a stack of file folders on the desk. The second thing he noticed were the two filing cabinets he recognized as coming from Tito Marcoletto's office.

The Director was reading the file in front of him, and as Fowler approached the desk, he flipped the folder shut and folded his hands on top of it.

Fowler set his bundle on the desk and unwrapped it. "Here are the plates, sir."

The paraffin had been boiled off, and the plates gleamed in the light from the banker's lamp. The reverse plate was intact. The obverse plate was bent inward around a .45 caliber dent in the steel.

"We'll all sleep better tonight. The President will be pleased. Excellent work, Agent Fowler."

"Thank you, sir."

"I'm recommending commendations for you, Kendall, and your team."

"Thank you, sir."

"What is the prognosis on Marcoletto?"

"Likely a full recovery. A life sentence for him should be a long one."

"I'll look forward to reading your full report."

"We've uncovered enough information on Marcoletto and his people to put them all away."

The Director grunted. "By the way, I've had some calls, people trying to run interference for him, but it won't come to anything. Apparently Marcoletto had compromising information on a large number of his customers." He waved a hand at the stack of files. "Now I have it."

"There's still the issue of the leak, how Moon, the hit man, knew what car I was driving. I don't think it came from here."

"Where, then?"

"I drove the car to Steinmetz Jewelry. Someone there may have seen it."

The Director nodded. "It will interest you to know that we have an eye on Steinmetz already. We suspect that he's an operative of the German government. There's a war coming in Europe, Agent Fowler. Mussolini is cozying up to Hitler. I wouldn't be surprised that Steinmetz was party to Marcoletto's plot."

The Director opened a drawer of his desk and drew out yet another file. "Perhaps you'd like me to make Gerhard Steinmetz your next assignment." He handed the file to Fowler.

"Thank you, sir."

"You'll be receiving a call from the Justice Department liaison. They want to discuss the Krasicki woman and her cooperation in the case."

"And Stroud?"

"He's turned State's Evidence, but he's in it so deep the best he'll do is watch everyone else go to the gas chamber through the bars of his cell."

There was a pause. The Director reopened the file he'd been reading. Dismissed.

Fowler turned as he was about to leave and saw something he had never seen before. On the Director's face as he pored over the file was a smile that would grace a child on Christmas morning.

THE END

SHINE OF THE MOON

(1)

A gent Dan Fowler opened his eyes and saw nothing.

He lay face down. A faint drift of chill air brushed his skin. Cold. It was cold. How could it be cold in the middle of September?

His cheek rubbed against dry, hard-packed grit. Sand? He couldn't be on a beach. There was no sound of surf. There couldn't be. He was in Southwestern Pennsylvania.

He tried to raise a hand to his face, and both moved together. They were tightly bound in front of him. He tried to move his feet and found them tied as well. He rolled onto his back and gasped as a white hot bolt of pain ripped though his skull.

New rule. Don't move your head.

When the pain subsided, Fowler opened his eyes again and saw only utter blackness. No stars, and even a quarter moon would have shown around the edges of clouds. He was indoors. He was a prisoner.

How did I get here? He thought.

Wherever here is.

A surge of panic welled up in him. He thrashed side to side for a moment, fighting to free himself. His pulse boomed in his ears. Deep breaths, he told himself. Deep breaths. Slowly, his heartbeat slackened and his breathing became normal. Time to quietly assess his circumstance.

Fowler took a deep breath through his nose, "tasting" the air. It was an earthy smell, but clean, crisp.

"Hey!" he shouted.

The sound was flat, much of it absorbed by the sand on the floor, and he thought of it as a floor. The short bounce of his voice told him he was in an enclosed space, but one with some elbow room.

No one shouted back. No one came.

He realized in a moment where he was.

He was in a cave.

At least it wasn't a grave.

He was lucky his captors tied his wrists in front of him and not behind. Fowler was able to reach the buckle of his belt. He opened it and twisted it counterclockwise. He tugged at it, and it slid from between the layers of leather, bringing a razor sharp blade with it. The Bureau's armorer had called it a "knife of last resort" when it was issued to all agents. Fowler figured this situation qualified.

It was tedious work sawing at the ropes that bound him. It involved difficult angles and movement, and more than once he had to stop to relieve cramping of his hands, but once the rope was cut through, he was able to work his bonds loose and his hands were free.

Next were the ropes at his ankles. Halfway through, he felt something scuttle over his thigh. Then another. Rats. He swatted them away, and they squeaked in protest at a meal that fought back.

One crawled up his thigh, and he stabbed it with his knife. The rat squealed and Fowler pressed it against his leg, plunging the blade deeper.

The impaled rat struggled and bit the agent's hand, but he held it until it stopped squeaking and squirming and threw it away from him, hoping fresh blood would draw the others away.

Freeing his feet was much easier than his wrists, and he quickly was done. They were numb and it took a good minute or two of stamping and rubbing before he felt the needles as his circulation returned.

Once he could stand, Fowler did so, slowly, an arm raised overhead to find the ceiling of the room before his aching head did. It was taller than his reach.

Time to take inventory. His pistols and shoulder rig were gone. He went through his pockets. No watch or wallet, including his badge, and his lighter was missing as were his cigarettes. In his back pocket he found a pair of paper napkins from the hotel's diner. It would be enough.

The aglets at the tips of Fowler's bootlaces hid tiny rods of flint. Strike one against the steel of his belt buckle and he could throw a spark that should catch the napkin on fire and give him some light for however brief a time.

He remembered going caving when he was a Boy Scout. Their guide took them deep into the earth and told them to blow out their candles. They did, and the darkness was as absolute as he'd ever seen. After waiting a moment for their pupils to fully dilate, the guide lit one match. The result was like the sun coming up.

Fowler crouched and tried striking a flint against the buckle. The spark was like a flashbulb going off, and it left a vivid image on his retina: a pile of skulls and bones.

He twisted one of the napkins into a tight cone. A few tries, and the tip caught, a faint orange glow. Fowler blew gently on it, and it flared. It would provide a minute of light, give or take. He looked around him for anything that would burn.

The grisly bone pile had scraps of ragged cloth, and some newer clothing. He took a piece of rag and dangled it over the burning cone. It was dry enough to catch. Before it burned out, Fowler chose a femur from the jumbled skeletons and wrapped a piece of cloth around one end. He lit it from the burning rag and the improvised torch showed him his surroundings.

He was in a room approximately thirty feet in diameter. The floor was dun-colored hard-packed sand, and the rough stone walls arched upward to meet fifteen feet above him. He turned slowly, holding the torch to the side so it wouldn't affect his vision. Behind him, he spotted the opening of a passage. The way out. But to where?

Time to find out.

(2)

Three days before, Fowler was summoned to the Director's office to find a man sitting in one of what his colleagues called the "Inquisition" chairs facing the desk. The visitor was trim, fit, hair grey at the temples. His suit was well tailored, and his Oxfords were spit shined; the epitome of the Federal law enforcement professional.

The Director sat on the power side of the desk.

"Sit down, Agent Fowler. This is Agent Joseph Keogh, ranking agent in the Treasury Department's Pittsburgh office." Keogh rose to shake Fowler's hand. His grip was firm and confident, but not bone-crushing. "Agent Keogh, please tell Agent Fowler what you just told me."

Fowler sat and Keogh began.

"Over the past ten months, three agents from our department's Bureau of Internal Revenue, Edward Pomeroy, William Zajac, and Eldon Biggs have disappeared in Fayette County, Pennsylvania. All were investigating moonshine operations, untaxed whiskey-making in the rural mountains."

"I would have thought that the Twenty-first Amendment would have ended the demand for home brew," Fowler said.

Keogh shook his head. "Not a bit. The demand has been there since Colonial times. In fact, Fayette County was the home of the Whiskey Rebellion, a violent tax protest in 1791 that lasted three years. Farmers found it cheaper and easier to convert their corn to whiskey for transport over the mountains to market. The Federal government imposed the Whiskey tax, and there the trouble began.

"A farmer named John Gaddis organized the protestors into a kind of militia, and they ran the tax collectors out of the county, often beaten, tarred, and feathered in the bargain. George Washington himself led a force of thirteen thousand men to suppress the rebellion."

"So, it's a local tradition to rough up the tax collectors?"

Keogh nodded. "Revenuers, they call them. The moonshine business has never been stamped out completely. Families have been in the trade for generations. The locals in the remote mountain areas are suspicious of outsiders, especially law enforcement, and they won't help. These people are very clannish. Most of them are related to one moonshiner or another, and they won't cooperate. Unfortunately, the same is true of the local sheriff and his deputies.

"Part of the problem is that during Prohibition, we were too busy chasing Capone and the bootleggers to prosecute the moonshiners. They got used to running around unhampered for years, and now that we're cracking down on them, they're retaliating."

"We're talking rustics, right? Jukes and Kallikaks."

"You mean hillbillies. Don't be fooled. These people are uneducated, but they're not stupid. They have a kind of feral cunning about them that substitutes for what they call 'book learnin'. The Depression has left them relatively untouched. In fact they've thrived in it. They've lived off the land for six or seven generations and they're fiercely protective of their way of life. Don't underestimate them, Agent Fowler. They're a dangerous breed."

"I'll remember that. Do you think that all three of these agents have been murdered by the same people?"

"Treasury has had agents killed before, but not so many in so short a time. We think that someone is trying to expand, maybe corner the market, and they want enforcement out of their way. The apparent urgency makes me think something big is about to happen, and we want to prevent it if we can."

"And how can I help?" Fowler said.

The Director said, "Treasury needs an agent who is not known to the locals to investigate." He looked pointedly at Keogh. "Investigate, not infiltrate."

"I agree. These are family operations," Keogh added. "The likelihood of you getting inside one of these moonshine rings is zero. Blood is the best security."

"Then how would you recommend I proceed?"

"To begin, I'll turn over all of our files on the case. We'll provide a regional agent as your liaison, David Porter. A standard investigation is out of the question; that's what got our people killed. I'll leave the procedure to your discretion."

Fowler turned to the Director, who gave a curt nod. "One question up front: who runs this show? Does Porter call the shots, or do I?"

Keogh hesitated. The Director stared across the desk at him and said, "Fowler runs the operation." Keogh opened his mouth to speak, and the Director said, "Non-negotiable," with the finality of a bank vault slamming shut.

"Very well," Keogh said,"if you insist."

"I do." The Director put his hands flat on his desk. "Thank you for coming in, Agent Keogh. Agent Fowler will study the files and make recommendations. I will then contact Secretary Morgenthau with my decision."

Keogh rose from his chair. Fowler began to rise also, and the Director said, "Please stay, Agent Fowler." He turned to Keogh. "It was a pleasure to meet you."

Fowler read the irony in the Director's tone, but if Keogh did, to his credit, he didn't let on. The Treasury Agent closed the door on the way out, but the Director waited a silent ten count to be sure Keogh was out of earshot.

"I want you to know that Secretary Morgenthau requested our aid in general, and he requested you in particular. He was impressed with your work on the Marcoletto case."

"That is very gratifying, sir."

"What it is… is a pain in my ass. I'm tired of these people expecting us to clean up their messes. Unfortunate, but the request came via the White House, and it's not so easy to refuse."

"I have a feeling that Keogh didn't tell me the whole story."

"Perceptive as always, Agent Fowler. Keogh didn't tell me either. Morgenthau suspects that someone on his team is fingering the agents sent from outside the region."

"Did Keogh have any ideas as to who?"

"None. That's why he wants the Bureau to have a hand in it."

"I'll review the files immediately. How soon do you want to make your decision?"

"I have already. You'll do it. I just don't want those piss-ants in Treasury to think we'll jump when they snap their fingers."

"Who will be working with me on this, sir?"

"It's a simple fact-finding mission. I'm sure you can handle it on your own. Review the files and we'll discuss any recommendations you have tomorrow morning."

"Yes, sir."

The Director rose from his chair and stood by the window, looking to the boulevard below.

Dismissed.

(3)

The drive to Fayette County was pleasant, through the rolling farmland and over the Allegheny Mountains on Route 40. Fowler passed into Pennsylvania in the early afternoon, scattered raindrops spotting the windshield of the Bureau's standard issue car, a blunt green '32 Pontiac sedan that he always thought looked like a shoebox on wheels. The Director authorized the purchase of a fleet of them.

Maybe Pontiac was the low bidder, which made sense. An automaker with a bunch of cars that unsightly would be happy to unload them from inventory. Fowler suspected, however, that the Director chose the model and color to remove the temptation from his people to drive The Big Uglies, as the agents nicknamed them, for personal use off the clock. Who would want to take his family or his sweetheart out on the town in one of those eyesores?

Route 40 was the first National Road, going back to Washington's day, and the same Route the moonshiners' forebears followed carrying corn liquor to market in Cumberland. And now the moonshiners were using the same road in their hopped up cars to transport illegal alcohol.

He imagined George Washington leading thirteen thousand troops along this same road to quell the Whiskey Rebellion and end the illegal whiskey business. But it never really stopped. It simply went underground for a century and a half. And Treasury expected to end it with a handful of agents.

The Appalachian mountain chain was ruggedly beautiful, borderline wild. Much of it was still first growth forest; pine, maple, and oak trees, and dense brush crowded either side of the highway as if they were waiting to pounce, to reclaim the narrow ribbon of land from the pavement.

Fowler recalled a lecture from his college days in which his professor discussed the origins of what he called the "Appalachian personality."

"During Colonial times," his professor had said, "England used the North American territories as an ad hoc penal colony, a dumping ground for its criminals and undesirables, similar to the use of Australia in the next century. They, along with people eager to escape indentured servitude and other misfits ran inland at their first opportunity and stopped at the first natural boundary, the Appalachian Mountains. There they took up residence in the forest where they couldn't be found and lived the way they wanted, free from the scrutiny and restraint of law, church, and society."

He went on, "To this day, they exist on the fringes, living lives that border on the tribal, shunning the framework of modern society in favor of their concept of freedom, which to us would seem libertine and degenerate."

"Clannish" was the word Keogh also used to describe the nature of the locals, a web of interrelated families that lived by their own code, maintaining an uneasy coexistence with the rest of the world. A pocket full of secrets.

Fowler was to rendezvous with Treasury Agent David Porter at a roadside restaurant called Turner's Inn a few miles east of Uniontown, the Fayette County seat. The restaurant, a stone building with a large chimney at either end, commanded a panorama of the valley spread below the mountains. Fowler stepped out of his coupe and stood for a moment admiring the view.

"Fowler?" a voice from behind.

He turned to see a compact man in a chambray work shirt and khaki trousers, arms folded, leaning against a dark blue Chevrolet coupe.

"Porter."

The man nodded. Fowler walked over to the Chevy, taking the man's measure as he did. Six feet two inches, a hundred eighty pounds, flat stomach and broad shoulders. His face was weathered and seamed, though he couldn't have been over forty; he was no desk jockey.

Porter chuckled. "That's the ugliest car I've seen in a while."

"It has its upside. I could leave it running with a sign on the windshield that says 'Free Car', and, nobody would take it," then quietly, "I'd shake hands, but we don't want to look like new acquaintances, do we?"

Porter laughed, showing a set of front teeth that would make a beaver proud. "That must be one of those fine points of undercover work they teach you guys at the Police Training School."

"Kept me alive so far. As I recall, during Prohibition you boys got a thorough education in the rough and tumble."

"In those days, they recruited us from the big city PDs instead of trying to teach the accountants and lawyers how to shoot. I was a detective in Reading when they asked me to sign on."

"I don't know about you," Fowler said, "but I've been driving all day and I'm hungry."

"Then let's go in."

Inside, the restaurant was fitted out like a nightclub with a low bandstand and a dance floor at one end. The place was almost empty, and the agents sat at a table away from the other customers. A bony waitress in a pale blue uniform with Monteen stitched on her breast and her dark hair in a snood scurried over. "What'll it be, gents?"

Fowler looked to Porter and raised an eyebrow.

"If you're on an expense account, I recommend the sirloin. If not, they make a good club sandwich."

Porter was right. The steak was excellent. Fowler followed his lead and ordered a bottle of Iron City beer. "Brewed in Pittsbugh," Porter said. It too was tasty.

"How long have you been here?"

"I came here two years ago."

"Must have taken a major cultural adjustment; City Mouse to Country Mouse."

"I can tell you, Fowler, it's a whole different way of life here in the mountains, like stepping back a hundred years. It's worse than the Wild West because there, people didn't sneak around. They wore their guns in plain sight."

"Three agents in ten months," Fowler said.

"Without a trace."

"That must make recruiting tough."

Porter turned his bottle in his fingers. "It's hard to swallow. One of those guys, Eddie Pomeroy was from my district, and he was a friend."

"Were the others, Zajac, and Biggs, from the outside?"

"Yeah. It was necessary. This is too small a community for locals to sniff around. If they aren't related, everybody assumes they're 'revenuers.' The rule of thumb around here is don't trust anyone new for the first ten years and still keep an eye on them for the next ten."

Porter's gaze drifted out the window to the valley below. "I can tell you there's a sentiment among plenty of us to declare outright war on the bastards, take them all out and we're guaranteed to get the guilty party, but the vests upstairs wouldn't hear of it."

"I'm sure it's frustrating. Has anyone suggested vigilante tactics?"

Porter's face hardened. "Is that an official question?"

Fowler shook his head. "Between us. I'm just getting the whole picture."

"There's been some talk. Kill one of them, legitimately or otherwise, every time they kill one of us. So far, it's come to nothing. I think that's why the Secretary called you guys in. He's afraid that it'll boil over and our people will use what we learned in the War to start another one."

"That might be satisfying," Fowler said, "but the risks are pretty stiff."

"You're right, but emotions muddy the clearest water. Truth be told, if we killed every moonshiner on the mountain, there'd probably be few men left over the age of ten."

...pine, maple, oak trees, and dense brush crowded either side of
the highway as if they were waiting to pounce...

"Who are the principal players?"

"Three big families: the Brickers, the Headleys, and the McCains. Of the three, the McCains run the biggest operation. Abner "Jumbo" McCain is the patriarch, and like all the family heads, he rules his clan with an iron fist. It's almost medieval."

"I understand the problem with catching them making the whiskey; it's a portable operation, but can't you intercept them during transport?"

"That poses a couple of problems. The woods are criss-crossed with one-lane dirt roads and overgrown cow paths. From any given still site, there are a dozen routes a runner could take. Complicating things, we don't have the manpower to watch for them twenty-four hours a day.

"Then there are the cars. They have hopped up engines and heavy suspensions to handle the weight, and these boys know how to drive them. They'd give Barney Oldfield a run for his money. They outrun the average chase car nine times out of ten. If we can't catch them with the goods, we can't arrest them. They see it as a game. The Shiners' attitude is 'catch me if you can.' Pure and simple. "

"What about roadblocks?"

"Like I said about twenty-four hours. If we get a tip a run is coming through a specific stretch at a specific time, we catch one once in a while, but not often. And when we do nab one of them, guys like Jumbo McCain and Mayfield Headley show up grinning to post bail in cash in front of us from a roll of bills as big as a baseball. Just letting us know we aren't making a dent in their enterprise."

"What about the State Police?"

"We're in a unique situation in this corner of the Commonwealth. From where we sit right now, you can drive south for ten minutes and be in West Virginia. You can drive fifteen minutes east and be in Maryland. State Police jurisdiction stops at the border. The local barracks will give us support raiding a still, or setting up a roadblock, but they can't help as much as they might like to in chase situations."

"I can see why you're frustrated."

"You have no idea how frustrated we all are."

Neither spoke for a moment. Monteen came to the table. "You fellows want anything else?"

"I think I'd like coffee," Fowler said.

"Me too," Porter added.

"Cream and sugar?"

"None for me," Fowler said.

Porter grinned. "Straight, no chaser."

The waitress nodded. "Gotcha." She strode away toward the kitchen.

"The home office says to give you carte blanche," Porter said. "How do you want to work this?"

"This is your backyard. I'd like to hear your ideas."

While Porter spoke, Monteen dialed the phone on the wall in the kitchen. "Hello?" A jukebox blared in the background.

"This is Monteen. There's a new one."

"You know what to do."

"Right."

Monteen was back quickly. The agents went silent while she poured the coffee. "Anything else? We got fresh apple pie right out of the oven."

"Sounds good," Porter said.

"Yeah, I'll have a piece too."

"Slice of cheese is only five cents extra."

"You should be selling used cars," Fowler said with a laugh. "Sure. Add the cheese."

As she scurried away, Fowler said, "I want to see the sites the agents were investigating when they disappeared. Is that possible without giving ourselves away?"

"We'll need a guide. We have an informant who can take us, but it's a risky business. They see you walking up on one of their stills in the woods; you're likely to catch a bullet. And the woods are full of booby traps. I'll make the arrangements."

"We'll wait until dark?"

"Nine o'clock should give us cover. Here comes the pie."

The pie was as good as the steak. They finished their coffee, and Fowler picked up the tab. At the cars, he said, "I've reserved a room at the Mount Summit Inn. You can contact me there."

"I'll call you. Dress for the great outdoors."

As they drove away, Monteen peered out the kitchen window at the departing cars. She jotted Fowler's license number on her order pad, stubbed out her cigarette, and fished in her pocket for another nickel for the phone.

(4)

The view from Turner's Inn was impressive, but it paled beside the panorama from the portico of the Summit. The big white Victorian hotel offered a view of the entire valley, unobstructed by the mountains. Fowler set down his suitcase and stood at the end of the pillared veranda. The forest was spread below like a rumpled green carpet. It was sad that such natural beauty masked the lawless rottenness underneath its verdant cover.

"They say you can see the lights of Pittsburgh on a clear night." An older gentleman stood at the railing. He was dressed in the kind of casual clothing fashion designers called "sport," but the average Joe called "expensive." Wire rimmed glasses perched on his bulbous nose. "Of course those nights are rare because of the damned coke ovens." Clouds of grey smoke hung in a dozen spots, like skeins of wool from dirty sheep.

"I suppose it's a trade off," Fowler said. "Smoke means work. Work means recovery. That means taking people off the dole."

The man snorted. "I suppose that's true, but I'd almost rather support them with my tax money than have the steel companies muck up nature. Did you know that George Washington once wrote that Redstone Creek down there at the foot of the mountains was the finest trout fishing in the Colonies?"

Fowler shook his head. "No, I never heard that,"

"If you looked at Redstone Creek now, you'd see it's yellow with sulfur and so poisoned with acid from the mines nothing could live in it."

Rather than engage in an argument over the relative importance of Humanity over Nature, Fowler tried to excuse himself by saying, "I'd better get checked in."

"Staying long?"

"A few days."

"Business or pleasure?"

The questions were getting intrusive. Fowler ignored him and picked up his suitcase. "Have a nice day, sir."

"Name's Montrose. J.B. Montrose. And yours?"

"Dan." Fowler turned and started walking before Montrose could extend the conversation. He passed a sign at the entrance that read PORCH SLEEPING 50 CENTS A NIGHT. He was glad the Bureau didn't know about that arrangement, or he'd probably be carrying a sleeping bag along with his suitcase.

The hotel interior was lavish, if a little worn by age and neglected because of the Depression. The lobby was spacious, offering reading chairs and sofas arranged around a rough stone fireplace at one end and around a baby grand piano at the other. Opposite the entrance, an oaken grand staircase climbed to the upper floors.

The registration desk stood to one side of the stairs, and a concierge desk to the other. Fowler registered and as the desk clerk handed him the key, Fowler noticed out of the corner of his eye that Montrose was walking by. Instinctively, he palmed the key fob, hiding the room number.

"If you need or want anything, please ring the desk," the clerk said, ringing the ornate brass call bell. "Front." A uniformed bellhop appeared from nowhere. Before the clerk could tell him the room number, Fowler showed the bellhop the key.

The hotel had no elevator, so Fowler followed him up the stairs to the third floor. Montrose didn't follow. The room was located at the end of the hallway, which pleased Fowler, since no one would have any legitimate reason to come as far as his door. Three missing agents was reason enough for caution. The bellhop opened the room with a passkey and carried the suitcase inside.

"May I get you anything, sir?"

"What's your first name, fellah?"

"Walter, sir."

"I'd like a newspaper, Walter, today's if it's available." Fowler slipped the bellhop a two dollar bill. "Keep the change."

"Thank you, sir." Walter slipped out and closed the door behind him.

Fowler had spent the night in plenty of hotel rooms and he had to admit this one was in the top five. The window had a southern exposure, looking into the towering trees behind the building. A deep clawfoot bathtub shared the private bath with the sink and toilet. He turned the hot water tap and counted only to twenty-eight before the cold water turned hot.

The poster bed was comfortable, and beside a wardrobe, an armchair stood next to a small table holding a reading lamp and a cathedral radio. Not bad, he thought, stretching out on the bed. Not bad at all.

Walter returned in a few minutes with The Evening Standard, and The Pittsburgh Press under his arm.

"Are you on duty tonight, Walter?"

"Yes, sir. My shift ends at one a.m."

"I'll ask for you if I need anything."

"Thank you, sir."

Fowler locked the door and set the burglar chain. He set his suitcase on the bed and opened it. He set out khaki duck trousers and a dark green turtleneck sweater. Lace-up steel-toed boots came out next and under them a pair of .45 automatics in a double shoulder holster.

Fowler took the pistols from the rig and one after the other went over them in detail, dropping the clip and dry firing each, then checking the slide, replacing the magazine and chambering a round. Never hurts to be safe, he thought. He set the pistols on the night stand and took a wind up alarm clock from the suitcase. He wound the clock, set the time by his watch, and just in case, set the alarm for eight o'clock. He stretched out on the bed, closed his eyes, and in a minute, he was asleep.

(5)

Fowler woke a few minutes before the alarm rang. He woke completely alert and swung his feet off the bed. In minutes, he was dressed and ready for the night's work. Outside, the sun had set, and the shadows were deepening from indigo to black. He opened the window. Outside, the air, which had been warm earlier, was turning chilly.

The phone on the nightstand rang. He picked up the receiver and before he could say hello, the voice on the other end said, "Fowler? It's Porter."

"Right."

"I'll meet you in the lobby in a half hour."

Fowler jiggled the hook on the receiver.

"Operator."

"This is Daniel Fowler in room 317. I need an outside line."

He dialed the D.C. exchange and Sally Vane's number. She answered on the fourth ring.

"Hello. This better be you, Fowler."

"It is, Sally."

Sally Vane was a rarity in the Bureau, a female agent. Openly resented by half the men and secretly admired by the other half, she strove to prove she wasn't just another curvy blonde. Her investigative skills were top shelf, and she could shoot and fight as well as most of her colleagues.

Despite the Bureau's prohibition against fraternization, she and Dan Fowler had become an "item." Everyone suspected it, but looked the other way. Dan would have married her without hesitation, but it probably would have ended her career.

"So tell me, Fowler, how's Pennsylvania?"

"Very green and very mean." For the next five minutes, he recounted his meeting with Porter and their plans for the evening.

"You be careful, Dan. Those people are as dangerous as the Mob, maybe more."

"It's just reconnaissance tonight, look don't touch."

"Promise me."

"I promise, Sally. I won't take any chances."

"You already are."

"I'd better hang up before the phone bill puts a deficit in the Federal budget."

"Call me tonight and let me know when you get back. It doesn't matter how late. I won't be sleeping til I know you're safe."

"I will."

"Okay." Sally hung up. The dial tone buzzed in his ear. Lately, when either of them was on assignment, she refused to say goodbye, afraid the word would jinx them, and the goodbye would be permanent.

Fowler hung up, slipped his jacket over his shoulder rig, and headed downstairs.

The Summit's coffee shop was open til ten. He took the stairs to the basement level and as he passed the empty lounge, he looked in the door. The bartender was doing his setup for the evening, and the four piece combo; piano, bass fiddle, trumpet, and drums, was warming up for the night's gig. The bass drum had the words Tune Toppers painted on its head arching over a top hat. Fowler stopped for a moment to listen. The pianist started a bouncy riff, and the bassist joined in. The drummer laid down a back beat with his brushes, and the trumpeter blew some jazzy riffs that would make Louis Armstrong proud.

They ran with it for a minute or two, then satisfied with their sound, ended with a crash from the cymbals. Fowler clapped. The bass player grinned and said, "Not bad for a pack of white boys huh?"

"Not bad at all."

"Come back at ten and we'll play you some real music."

Fowler gave him a two-finger salute and walked away, wishing he could stick around like an everyday person, just an average Joe with a beer and his girl enjoying some good music. But not tonight.

The coffee shop was open but empty. Eight stools at the counter and four tables with café chairs and red and white checkered tablecloths. No one was behind the counter, but Fowler could hear pots and pans rattling on the other side of the wall.

He took a stool and waited a minute, and when no one appeared, he said, "Hello."

A head appeared in the pass through window. "Be right there, Chief." A man in kitchen whites came behind the counter wiping his hands on a rag. "Sorry. My counter girl called off sick. I'm the whole show tonight. What'll you have?"

"Just coffee."

"Coming up." He disappeared into the kitchen and came back with a cup and saucer and a carafe of steaming coffee. "Cream or sugar?"

"No thanks. I drink it black."

"Me too. Why water it down? For my money, it ain't coffee unless it climbs out of the cup and comes after me."

"I agree." Fowler laid a fifty cent piece on the counter. "Keep the change."

"Thanks. If you don't need anything else, I got a sink full of pots to wash."

Fowler waved him away. As he drank his coffee, he thought about Porter's odd remark about coffee to Monteen, the waitress, "straight, no chaser." She didn't blink or ask for an explanation. Maybe she heard him say it before.

He was wiping his mouth with a napkin when a voice from the coffee shop doorway said, "Fowler." He turned and saw Porter standing in the corridor. As an afterthought, he took two napkins from the chromed dispenser on the counter and tucked them in his pocket.

Porter was dressed as he had been earlier with the addition of a dun canvas hunting coat and a baseball cap. "Ready for a moonlight stroll?"

"All set."

"We have to pick up Phipps."

"Phipps?"

"Calvin Phipps. Our tour guide for the evening. We'll take your car. The whole County knows mine."

Outside, a near full moon beamed down on the rags of mist rising from the valley. "I'm glad it's a clear night," Fowler said.

"I agree. Sometimes the fog up here is so dense you can't see the end of your nose. I wouldn't even try if it was like that."

(6)

A few miles down the highway from the hotel, Porter said, "There's a dirt road coming up on the right in about three hundred yards. Pull in and cut the lights."

Fowler parked the Pontiac under a clump of trees whose dense branches blocked the moonlight. He shut off the headlights and the forest darkness closed around them like a velvet drape.

"So, tell me about this Phipps."

"Calvin's a local boy, born and bred. He was a moonshine runner, drove for Jumbo McCain til Jumbo found out Calvin was banging his daughter Lula. Jumbo's pretty smart. He knew if he killed Calvin, or beat him half to death, he'd make him a martyr and Lula would never give up on him.

"Calvin made a run to Hagerstown, and when he got to the drop-off site, my boys were waiting for him. We all figured Jumbo phoned in the anonymous tip. He put on a good show, posted Calvin's bail and footed the bill for his lawyer. 'The cost of doin' business,' Jumbo always said. Of course the lawyer, working for Jumbo, bungled the case, and Calvin was out of circulation for four years.

"By the time he got out of the Pen, Lula was married to a guy Jumbo picked out for her and had two kids. So much for romance. We pay him for info, but as far as Calvin's concerned, it's all about revenge."

Five minutes later, Fowler saw the glow of a cigarette twenty yards away. He heard a low three note whistle like a bird call. Porter answered it with the same notes. "There's our boy. Turn on your headlights."

Calvin Phipps stepped from a clump of mountain laurel. He was tall and rangy and looked to be mostly skin, bone, bone, and gristle. His dark hair was cut in a soup bowl style to his shaggy eyebrows. His head was bent forward, and his blue eyes stared from the tops of his sockets. His open unsmiling mouth showed both rows of his teeth, giving his face the look of a wary animal. He was dressed in oil stained dungarees and an unbuttoned work shirt over long underwear. A dun canvas barn coat completed his ensemble.

"Evening, Calvin. Get in."

"Money first." Calvin's voice had a whiny, nasal tone that sounded to Fowler like a petulant child.

Porter pulled a wad of folded bills from his shirt pocket and handed them out his window. Calvin held the money in front of the headlights as he counted it.

"What's the matter, Calvin? Don't you trust me?"

"Not even in the daylight."

"Behave, Calvin, or I'll tear up that nice letter I wrote to your parole officer. I haven't put the stamp on it yet." Calvin swore under his breath and climbed into the back seat. He gave off a smell that blended his body odor with tobacco smoke and axle grease. Fowler could only imagine his breath.

"Who's this fella?"

"Dan." No last names or pedigree. "So what do you have for us tonight, Calvin?"

"Jumbo's cookin' mash over't Hammet's Mountain." Like most of the locals, Calvin dropped his Gs and slurred his words together. "Big wreck bottom of the mountain today."

"Is that so?" Porter said.

"Yes, indeed. Truckload of chickens. Driver burned his brakes out on the grade. Musta been doing ninety when he went off the road near the bottom and hit one of them big elms on the side." He cackled. "Feathers everywhere. Word got out quick, and people swarmed in like locusts grabbing live birds and dead ones, like the quail in the Wilderness. Lots of people in Hopwood eatin' chicken tonight."

Fowler imagined Calvin as a little boy sitting in a church pew, face scrubbed clean and hair slicked back, next to his momma while his daddy slept off Saturday night; forced to listen to some hellfire preacher rant about the Israelites for an hour every Sunday then going back to business as usual the rest of the week. Apparently some of it stuck, just not enough.

"And the driver?" Porter said.

"They oughta just bury the cab of the truck." He snorted. "Have a hell of a time digging him out of the dashboard."

Fowler started the car. "Which way?"

"Turn right onto the highway," Phipps said. "I'll tell you from there."

For the next fifteen minutes, Calvin directed Fowler through a series of back roads and lanes, some paved and some not, some little more than the width of the car, branches and brush dragging along the doors and fenders.

"There's a clearing up ahead. Park it. We'll walk from there."

Fowler shut off the engine and cut the lights. The near full moon was high now, and its silvery light painted stark shadows under the canopy of leaves.

Porter climbed out. "Got a spare key for this heap?"

"Yeah, just in case."

"We always leave a key on the right front tire. You never know what might happen out here in nowhere land."

Fowler nodded and fished a key from his pocket. "Sounds sensible." He handed the key to Porter and switched on his pocket torch, checking the batteries.

"You might as well leave that here," Calvin said. "You won't be able to use it. Jumbo's boys see a light, they'll use it for target practice. We're lucky it rained a little today. No dry leaves to crunch underfoot." He turned to Fowler. "You ever hunt deer?"

"No." But plenty of men, he thought.

"That's okay. Just follow me close. Step where I do. Don't drag your feet; pick 'em up and set 'em down easy so you can feel twigs and roots underfoot." He turned to Porter. "You ready?"

"Lead the way."

"Let's go."

Fowler closed one eye to allow its pupil to dilate so that there would be no temporary blindness when they stepped from the moonlight into the dark. He and Porter followed Calvin's example and held a hand edgewise in front of their faces, thumb to nose to prevent branches from poking them in the eye.

Calvin moved carefully but quickly along the trail, his steps all but silent. He was obviously a seasoned woodsman and made Fowler, right behind him, feel clumsy by comparison. Porter too moved through the darkened forest without difficulty.

Like water following the path of least resistance, the trail snaked around the thick boles of the trees and outcroppings of limestone that seemed to boil out of the ground at random. The little moonlight that filtered through the dense canopy of leaves made an eerie chiascuro of what in daylight would have been a peaceful sylvan scene.

Fowler recalled the class in night operations the Bureau required for all its agents. The instructor told them that the psychological effect of night increases with the degree of darkness and that in general, men with rural backgrounds adjust more easily than do urban operatives. This certainly rang true with Calvin.

"Darkness stimulates the imagination," the instructor had said, "and taxes the nervous system. It can lead to a sense of insecurity, possibly even panic."

Something moved in the dense brush to their left, and Fowler instinctively reached for one of his pistols. Calvin held up a hand in a restraining gesture. "Deer," he whispered, almost inaudible. The men heard a sharp snort followed by the sound of hooves trotting easily through the laurel.

Calvin led them down another intersecting path, and Fowler realized the difficulty he'd have finding his way to the car on his own. He was in an outdoor labyrinth with no "clew of thread" to follow back. He felt uneasy, vulnerable, and glad his guns were handy.

They had been walking along a ridge, and the new path led them down the mountainside. The trail became steep, the footing difficult. Fowler wanted to reach out for a tree limb or a bush to steady himself but was afraid of the noise he might make. The moon was behind the mountain now, leaving them in almost total darkness.

Fowler felt the sticky silk of a spiderweb and frowned in disgust as he wiped the strands from his hand and face, hoping the spider didn't hitch a ride on his jacket.

The lovely peace of the Allegheny mountains concealed a wealth of perils; predators such as bears and cougars, poisonous snakes including timber rattlers, copperheads, and cottonmouth moccasins; and of course, poisonous spiders: wolf spiders, brown recluses, and black widows, whose venom was as much as fifteen times more potent than a rattlesnake's. Fowler gritted his teeth and pressed on; wondering how Calvin had dodged the web in the darkness and whether he'd intentionally let him walk into it just for laughs.

A night wind kicked up, rustling the branches, and on it, Fowler smelled a faint, sweetish odor mixed with wood smoke and alcohol. They were getting close.

A few yards down the path, Calvin stopped. He'd led them to the edge of a shelf of rock overlooking a clearing and hunkered down behind a stand of ferns. Fowler crouched beside him and peered through the foliage.

In the clearing twenty feet below he saw a pair of copper boilers, at least two hundred gallons each, standing over beds of coals that cast a hellish crimson glow over the scene. Coils of copper tubing snaked from the boilers and opened onto steel tanks alongside them. In the red glow, Fowler could make out the shapes of men some standing, some sitting with their backs against the trees. Six that he could see, probably more around the site, standing guard.

A stakeside truck was parked at the clearing's edge. It looked new. The moonshine business must pay well, he thought. The equipment wasn't cheap.

Calvin stood, and to Fowler's surprise, whistled his three note signal.

Porter said, "What the hell?"

Before Fowler could rise, Calvin brought a blackjack down across the back of his skull. White starbursts flashed across his vision, then blackness.

Porter snarled, "Are you crazy? What's wrong with you? This isn't the plan."

"Plan's been changed."

"To what? We were supposed to let him have a look where he couldn't find it again so he could go home and report, let things cool down a little."

"Jumbo said take him down."

"What was he thinking? This is going to take us all down, Calvin."

"Maybe. Maybe not." Calvin rolled the unconscious Fowler face up and took him by the shoulders. "You take his legs."

(7)

Jumbo McCain sat at a table made of rough hewn planks across a pair of saw horses. The table was empty except for a hurricane lamp and a two-eared jug.

The nickname fit. Giant was another word that suited him. Standing six-foot-seven and weighing over three hundred pounds, little of it fat, even seated Jumbo was an imposing presence. He was way short of Goliath's six cubits and a span, but what he lacked in height, he made up in attitude.

A leonine mane of white hair topped a head the size of a pumpkin. Bright green eyes shone below eyebrows that grew together over a long Roman nose, eyes that radiated power, intelligence, and menace. A full beard like the blade of a shovel hung to his chest.

Porter sat on a keg on the other side. Fowler lay unconscious on the floor beside him. "He was carrying these." Porter set Fowler's shoulder rig with its twin automatics on the table.

Jumbo took one of the pistols from its holster. It looked like a toy in his fist. "What else?" McCain's voice rumbled like a rolling barrel.

Porter put Fowler's wallet, his wristwatch, his badge and the other contents of his pockets on the table. Jumbo shook a Lucky Strike from Dan's pack and put it in his mouth. He raised the chimney of the lamp and lit the cigarette from its flame. He took a long drag, held it a second and blew the smoke out his nose.

"Daniel Fowler, FBI," he read from the agent's I.D. Jumbo's eyes shifted to Porter. "How much does he know?"

"I didn't tell him much of anything. I just –"

Jumbo's hand slammed the table, making Porter jump. "I don't mean what you told him, idiot. What did he know before he got here?"

"Not much. Just whatever Treasury had in its files."

"You see those files?"

Porter shook his head. "No, sir."

"Did he bring them with him?"

"I don't know."

Jumbo rummaged through the pile of Fowler's belongings. He picked up a brass key and turned it over in his thick fingers. He threw it on the table in front of Porter. "Time to find out."

"Look, Jumbo, Mister McCain, this puts me in a really tight spot. I take an FBI agent on a recon mission, I come back and he doesn't. What do I tell my boss? What do I tell the FBI?"

Jumbo pulled a .32 revolver from under his vest and shot Porter in his left arm.

"Tell them a good story."

Porter stared at Jumbo. Blood seeped between his fingers as he clutched his bicep. "You shot me," he said, incredulous.

"I just grazed you. Now get to it before I change my mind and shoot your head instead."

Porter stumbled out of the room and in a moment, a door opened behind Jumbo. Montrose stepped out.

Jumbo wore a smug grin. "What do you think?"

The little man took off his glasses, blew a breath on them and wiped the lenses with a handkerchief. "You should have discussed this with me, McCain. You may have made a mistake, overplayed your hand."

Jumbo pulled the cork from the jug and tipped it back, taking a long pull. He offered it to Montrose. "Drink?"

Montrose's lip curled. "I wouldn't touch it. You know, killing a G Man isn't the same as taking out one of those Treasury boys. We don't have a helper like Porter in the Bureau. They'll send more agents up here, I guarantee it."

"Let them come. They won't find shit. His car's on the bottom of Cheat Lake by now."

"Maybe you should lay low for a couple weeks. Let things cool off a little."

Jumbo's affable grin slipped away. His brows lowered as he rose from his seat and towered over Montrose. He sneered. Nobody told Jumbo McCain how to run his business. "I'll think about it."

Montrose was unintimidated. "Do that. Boston doesn't take kindly to people jeopardizing their investments, McCain. Think about that too." Montrose walked out without closing the door.

"Calvin!"

Phipps sauntered in with another man in overalls and a plaid wool jacket. "Yeah, Boss?"

Jumbo jerked his chin at the unconscious agent. "Take him below."

"Do you want me to shoot him? He's still breathing."

"Don't kill him. I may need him alive later."

The men lifted Fowler and carried him through the door behind Jumbo, leaving him alone. Jumbo took the second pistol from its holster and stood up, one in each fist. He held them out in front of him as if he were posing for the cover of a dime novel.

He'd have to get Haines, the saddle maker in Farmington, to fix him up a dual shoulder rig like Fowler's. Yeah, he thought, these pistols will suit me just fine.

Sally Vane set down the book she'd been reading, Fitzgerald's *Tender is the Night*. The tragic story of Dick Diver was engaging until the clock ticked past four a.m. and she started to really worry. Plenty of nights Dan had been out overnight on one case or another; it was part of the job. But those instances were, if not routine, at least within the Bureau's regular purview.

In her eyes, putting Dan in the wilds of Pennsylvania was no different than dropping him into the African Bush. He had support from Porter, the Treasury liaison who knew the turf and the players, but bottom line, Dan was out there on his own in a hostile environment. He's the best agent in the Bureau, she told herself. There's nobody more likely to walk into danger and come back with that lopsided grin on his face.

Sally started reading again. In five minutes, she gave up. She'd started the same page three times and lost her concentration. She switched off her bedside lamp and rolled on her side, but instead of closing her eyes, she stared into the darkness, listening for the jangle of the telephone.

(9)

Fowler tried to remember what he'd learned about caves in his college days in Geology I, but didn't remember much. His throbbing head didn't help. Being sapped made concussion a distinct possibility.

Time to take inventory. With no mirror to check his eyes, Fowler had no way to compare his pupils for relative size. He was able to walk with no balance issues. He felt a little light headed at first, but that passed quickly.

He hadn't puked up supper, which was a good sign, and his vision was clear; no blurring. He had a lump the size of a hen's egg over his left ear, which also was good, at least in one sense. If the swelling was on the outside, it was less likely to be swelling on the inside.

There was a slight ringing in his ears, but no "train whistles" as his partner Larry Kendall once described his concussion. In balance, Fowler likely didn't have one, just the mother of all headaches.

In the flickering torchlight, he saw dun colored sand hard packed on the cave floor. Overhead the brown limestone walls angled upward to meet in the middle like hands with steepled fingers.

A "solution cave" as the Geology professor described it, went back to prehistoric times when the mideastern U.S. was under the ocean. Water seeped through cracks in the bedrock, reacted with carbonate in the limestone, and dissolved it, leaving angular passages with sandy floors.

Fowler also recalled that the average temperature underground hovered around fifty-two degrees Fahrenheit. Porter and Phipps left him dressed as he was. If he stayed dry, hypothermia was no immediate concern.

Rummaging through the bones, Fowler counted at least twenty skulls. This must be where Jumbo disposed of inconvenient corpses. Three were fresher than the others, likely Pomeroy, Biggs, and Zajac.

He found nothing of use. The killers had taken anything of value or weapon potential, leaving only rags. Judging by the state of the bones, some as brown as walls of the cave, Fowler decided that the cavern had been the McCain family's charnel house for generations.

On the limestone wall, someone had used the flame from a carbide lamp to write the letters RIP in stark black script, either in superstition or as a ghoulish joke.

Fowler pocketed some rags for his makeshift torch and set off through the mouth of the passage. The silence of the cave was disturbed only by the distant drip of water and the occasional scuttling of the rats. He wondered at the absence of bats then remembered it was probably still night and they wouldn't return til dawn. Just as well.

He figured he wasn't too deep in the cave because Jumbo's men had to carry him, and he was no light load. All he had to do was find the right passage, but that would be no easy trick. The one he followed opened into a larger room with three tunnels spurring away in different directions like the clawfoot of a chicken.

The sand was packed so hard, that Fowler couldn't make out footprints. He decided to try each of the tunnels in turn, starting with the rightmost.

A secret to navigating a maze is keeping one hand consistently on the wall maintaining contact through every twist, turn and intersection, preventing doubling back. Fowler entered the first passage with his left hand on the rough limestone. He held the torch high and slightly behind his head to keep the glare out of his eyes, almost as bright to his dilated pupils as direct sunlight.

The spur was fairly straight and simple to follow, but the further he went, Fowler found the passage narrowing, and the roof lowering to the point he could barely pass through it, let alone two men carrying a body.

One down.

He turned around and found his way back to the passage's beginning.

The middle tunnel curved leftward. A good hundred feet into it, the path

Sally started reading again.

was blocked by a spider's web that reached wall to wall, floor to ceiling. The web was too large to have been spun in the last few hours.

That left number three.

The leftmost passage began the size of the others and maintained a fairly uniform width and height. Fowler followed it. The floor sloped gently upward, and he soon found himself in another room. Instead of the angular reach for the ceiling, this room was basically square, its ceiling flat, shored up with timbers like a mine tunnel. This room was excavated, carved out of the limestone decades before.

Crates lined one wall, stacked head high. Burlap bags of corn and sacks of sugar were piled against another. The cave was some sort of warehouse. He had to be close to the exit.

Something moved in a shadowy corner. Fowler's head swiveled, setting off a wave of pain that made him gasp. Eyes glowed in the torch light, then a half dozen furry shapes darted across the room almost too fast for Fowler to see that they were cats left to guard the corn from the vermin.

Beyond the room was another short passageway. At its end, Fowler found a heavy oaken door, thick slabs of wood bound with iron, hanging on old hammer-forged strap hinges. He saw a metal plate with a keyhole and a pull ring on the left side of the door. Setting down the torch, he crouched and put his ear to it.

Silence. He listened intently for a good minute and then he put his eye to the keyhole.

On the other side of the door was another man-made room. The wick was turned down in a kerosene lamp on a rough table, and Fowler couldn't see much, but on the other side of the room, he saw another iron-bound door. It had to be the way out.

He took a deep breath, grabbed the iron ring and gently tugged at it. The door didn't budge. He pulled harder. No luck. Without tools or a stick of dynamite, there was nothing Fowler could do but wait.

The cold in the cave was making his hands stiff. He retreated to the storeroom and warmed his hands over the flame of the torch. The cold was also draining his energy. He wanted to just lie down and close his eyes for a minute, but he knew what would happen; he'd never open them again. He couldn't risk even sitting down.

Then there were his captors. The lamp was burning, which meant someone was coming back. Eventually, someone would open that door, and when he did, Fowler had to be awake and ready with a plan.

(10)

Montrose pulled his car into the gravel lot of a diner and he parked beside a phone booth. He opened the glove compartment and took out a handful of change. You didn't call the number he was calling collect.

McCain had become a problem, and what to do about him was a decision beyond Montrose's authority. McCain had started the arrangement with the Boston families congenial and cooperative, glad for their backing in exchange for a cut of his profits, but over the last few months, he'd become arrogant and defiant instead of deferential, his true nature surfacing.

Montrose dialed O.

"Operator."

"I'd like to place a call to Boston, Massachusetts please." He rattled off the number from memory.

"Seventy-five cents for the first three minutes, sir."

Quarters jangled in the phone. Two rings and the call was answered.

"Yeah?"

"Montrose."

"Hang on."

In a moment, another voice came on the line. "What?"

Montrose recounted the incident with Fowler and Porter. "McCain seems to have delusions of grandeur. He's become a loose cannon."

"Can he be replaced?"

"It's a family operation. I doubt we could get one of his kin to turn on him. If we kill McCain, there'll be chaos and disruption."

"And if we let him live, there may be chaos and disruption anyway. This needs to be discussed. Call tomorrow night." The line went dead.

Montrose put the phone on the hook. *The gall of that hillbilly,* he thought, *thinking he can scare me. When the word comes down, I'll pull the trigger on him myself —with great pleasure.*

(11)

Sally sat up in bed and switched on the light. Five-thirty, and still no word from Dan. He gave her the Summit Hotel's phone number when he called earlier. She dialed O and in a minute the phone was ringing in Pennsylvania.

"Mount Summit Inn. How may I help you?"

"Would you please ring room 317 for me?"

"Yes, ma'am."

The phone rang eight times, ten, twelve. No answer. Sally hung up. She dialed Larry Kendall's number. He answered on the third ring.

"Hello?" His voice was thick with sleep.

"Larry, it's Sally Vane. Have you heard from Dan?"

"No. Why?"

Sally recounted her conversation with Fowler about his meeting with Porter and their plans for the evening. "He said he'd call when he got back. He hasn't. I rang his room at the hotel, and he didn't answer."

"He may still be out in the field. You know the official protocol is twenty-four hours before we declare an agent missing. Is there a reason you think he's in trouble?"

"Not specifically. It's just that he's by himself in that place. Why did they send him alone?"

"He's not alone, Sally. He's got the local liaison from Treasury working with him. And no matter what the situation, my money's on Dan. Give it a few more hours. He'll be all right. I'm sure of it."

"Okay, Larry. I'll be patient. Sorry I bothered you."

"Youre never a bother, Sally. If I thought Dan was in danger, I'd be in the car driving up there already. I understand your concern, but I really think he's okay. Call me when you hear from him."

"I will." Sally hung up the phone. Call me, Dan, she thought. Please be all right.

(12)

Fowler wrapped his arms around himself to stay warm. The rags he'd taken for his makeshift torch were almost gone. Light was no problem now, since he found a pair of kerosene lanterns hanging near the door.

Waking as he had in the dark with no way to reference time, Fowler had no way of knowing whether he'd been in the cave for three hours or ten. But, sooner or later, the moonshiners would need their supplies and come for them.

He cursed himself for falling into the trap Porter laid. The whole business started the minute they met. Porter's coffee comment was a signal to the waitress that set the whole plot in motion.

The story of Calvin's hatred for Jumbo McCain was probably bogus, but he bought it all. Keogh was right in his suspicion. Apparently Porter was the Judas, and Keogh needed the Bureau to smoke him out. Fowler cursed Porter for his duplicity and Keogh as well for his reticence or ignorance. It didn't matter which.

The temperature wasn't freezing, but the prolonged cold was seeping into Fowler's bones. Sooner or later, he'd experience low grade hypothermia, shivering and confusion, then slip into unconsciousness and the game was over. At least he was dry. Otherwise he might be dead already.

Dry. That was another issue. His tongue felt like sandpaper against the roof of his mouth. There was no water dish or food left for the feral cats that guarded the corn and sugar. Not feeding the cats forced them hunt for their supper, making them more aggressive in dealing with the rats, but they must have some source of water close by. They were probably sizing him up as a potential meal, but if things got that far, it wouldn't matter anymore.

Fowler's ears caught a faint sound. Voices, muffled but audible. Someone was coming.

He doused the lamp and quietly moved behind the mound of corn sacks, clutching the thigh bone in his right fist and his knife in the other. It was time to save himself or die trying.

He heard the rattle of the lock and the groan of the iron hinges. Light.

"Ah, hell. Where's the other lamp?"

Fowler recognized Calvin's whining drone.

"Don't need but one." A second voice. "I been down here so many times I could find my way in the dark."

"Yeah, sure you could, Andy. Let's get this over with."

"What's Jumbo want Mister FBI for anyway?"

"Jumbo don't give reasons, just orders."

Only two of them. Fowler heard the hinges again, and the door slammed shut. No jangle of keys. They left it unlocked. The bobbing light of the lantern threw dancing shadows on the walls. Fowler raised his arm and held his breath.

The lantern passed his hiding place. Calvin was leading the way, holding it casually at his side. Andy ambled two steps behind him. Short and stocky, he looked like a scrapper. His hands were empty. Take him first. Fowler waited until Andy was a stride past him and stepped out of hiding.

He swung the bone in a wide arc and caught Andy just ahead of his right ear. The hit was solid, and Fowler could feel Andy's skull give under the impact.

Calvin spun around, and Fowler caught him in the jaw backhanded. Calvin dropped the lantern and staggered backward out of Fowler's reach for a second blow. Calvin reached under his coat, and Fowler was almost relieved when he pulled out a wicked looking Bowie knife instead of a gun. The blade flashed in the harsh light. Calvin snarled like an animal and lunged at Fowler, blade first.

Fowler swung for Calvin's knife hand, but found it was like swinging at the head of a coiled rattlesnake. The hand twitched away at the last second, and Calvin stepped in to punch Fowler on the tip of his chin, setting off a wave of white pain in the agent's head.

Calvin kicked the club from the Fowler's hand, and he staggered backward, still holding his short bladed knife. Calvin's lip curled back in a sneer. "Jumbo said bring you back, FBI man. He didn't say in what shape. So pull out your pecker and let's see whose is bigger."

Calvin saw Fowler's knife and laughed. "That's all you got, FBI? This is gonna be fun." He stepped in and slashed at Fowler, who raised an arm to block him. The blade sliced through the agent's sweater and Fowler felt a hot jolt of pain.

His foot lashed out, and he caught Calvin in the knee. Calvin grunted in pain and tottered for a second, giving Fowler a chance to get out of reach between him and the lantern. Fowler felt blood soaking his sleeve.

"I don't give damn what Jumbo says," Calvin snarled. "I'm gonna gut you like a yearling." He lunged at Fowler, and as he did, the agent scooped up the lantern and swung it at Calvin's head. The glass shattered, and the lantern doused Calvin with flaming oil.

He screamed and spun around, arms flailing as his hair caught making his head a ball of flame. He screamed once more, bounced off one wall of the passage then the other and fell face down, where he lay still.

Fowler's head spun. He sat for a moment, his back against the passage wall, composing himself. He relit his lantern. Calvin's Bowie knife lay beside him. The handle had three notches cut into it. Fowler would have been the fourth. Calvin wasn't moving. He'd likely inhaled the flames and seared his lungs and windpipe.

He searched the dead man's pockets and was disappointed to find no gun, but he found a ring of keys, two he recognized as the odd shape of Fords.

A sound behind him. He turned to see Andy struggling to raise himself on his hands and knees. Blood ran out his ear. He shook his head like a wet dog.

Fowler scooped up the thigh bone and clubbed the back of his head once, twice, three times. Andy sank to the sand. Fowler showed no mercy. These animals left him to be eaten alive by rats. He rolled Andy face up with his foot. Blood ran from both his ears now. Fowler raised his club over his head and brought it down with both hands in the middle of Andy's forehead. The blood stopped flowing.

A search of Andy came up with a cheap over-under Derringer. Fowler broke it open. Two shots, .32 caliber. A belly gun, its short barrels inaccurate to aim at any distance.

Better than nothing.

Fowler pulled himself to his feet and rolled back the cuff of his sweater. Calvin had cut his forearm pretty deep. He'd need stitches and a tetanus shot for sure. God only knew where Calvin's knife had been. But first, he had to get out and get away.

He knelt by the door and put his eye to the keyhole. Nothing moved. With Andy's Derringer in one hand and Calvin's Bowie in the other, Fowler pulled the ring. The door opened a crack. He peered through it and saw a room with a table and empty chairs. He entered cautiously and saw the jug on the table beside the lamp.

He set his weapons down and uncorked the jug. He poured the moonshine on his forearm and grunted at the burning pain of almost pure alcohol. Against his better judgment, he put the jug to his lips, tilted it back, and took a drink. The moonshine was like swallowing lava, and his empty stomach almost puked it up, but in a moment, his pain subsided. Time to make a move.

(13)

Outside the cave, Porter waited with Wilbur, one of Jumbo's men, who leaned nonchalantly against the shiny new stakeside truck, a sawed off pump shotgun in the crook of his arm and a cigarette dangling from his lips.

It was nearly dawn, and Porter was exhausted, His arm throbbed from the gunshot. Jumbo was crazy, but his logic made sense. Porter could say they were caught snooping around a still, there was a gunfight, he was lucky, and

Fowler wasn't. Who's to say otherwise?

What Porter didn't agree with was the way Jumbo arbitrarily changed the plan without warning. But Jumbo was Jumbo, as Porter learned in the three years he'd been on the moonshiner's payroll. It worried him enough that the FBI was pulled into the case, but Fowler's disappearance doubled his anxiety. He'd go under the hot lights, but if he held his nerve, he believed he could finesse even the best of Treasury's and the FBI's investigators. With Fowler dead, there was no one to contradict his story.

He needed a cigarette. The pack in his shirt pocket was empty, but he had a deck of Camels in his coupe, parked behind the truck. He was reaching under the seat when the door to the cave swung open.

No one came out. Wilbur reached for his cigarette and before his hand reached his mouth, Fowler bolted through the doorway, Derringer in hand. He pulled the trigger and the mechanism of the cheap pistol fired both barrels at once as Wilbur swung the shotgun around, jacking a shell into the chamber.

One shot caught him in the shoulder, and the other, to Fowler's good luck went through his throat and out the back of his neck. Wilbur dropped the shotgun and clutched his throat, blood spurting between his fingers.

Porter drew his automatic and jumped out of the coupe. He fired as Fowler scooped up Wilbur's shotgun. Fowler returned fire, blowing the windshield out of Porter's car.

Fowler yanked the door of the truck open as Porter's bullets whanged off its body. He climbed in and pushed the key marked Ford into the ignition, praying it was the right one. Porter slammed a new clip into his pistol as the truck's engine caught.

Fowler threw the truck into reverse and popped the clutch. He swung the wheel hard right and the truck heeled around in a tight arc to smash into the fender of Porter's coupe, crushing it into the tire. The truck roared away, leaving Porter cursing.

He opened the trunk and pulled out the jack handle to pry the fender away from the tire. He was lucky it wasn't blown in the bargain. He'd be going again in a minute. There was only one way out of the hollow, and Porter figured he'd catch Fowler before he got away. He had to. It was his ass if he didn't.

Fowler steered the truck over the rutted logging road as fast as he dared, sure at any moment he'd blow a tire, break an axle, or rip off the oil pan on the chunks of rock that dotted the unpaved surface. Lucky for him the truck was jacked up for better clearance. On either side of the road, the treeline was unbroken.

He felt as if he might puke or pass out as the bouncing truck threw him from side to side. The pain in his head throbbed with every jolt. He gripped the wheel desperately so he wasn't thrown around the cab like a beach ball.

The trees thinned out in a mile or so, but the road wasn't much better. To his right he saw brief glimpses of the highway running parallel. If his luck held, he'd be on it in a few minutes and find help.

The side mirror exploded, showering Fowler with shards of glass. He looked in the rearview mirror and saw Porter's coupe lurching through the ruts close behind him.

Fowler looked again to his right and saw a break in the trees a hundred feet ahead where power lines crossed the highway. He wrenched the wheel and the truck heaved out of the ruts and crashed through the thick brush. The highway was at least ten feet below the level of the ground Fowler was covering, which ended in a wooded bank too steep and too close to drive down.

He floored the gas pedal, and in seconds, the truck was airborne, perpendicular to the pavement. It came down hard on all four wheels in the westbound lane and bounced. The driver's door flung open, and Fowler was nearly thrown from the cab, but he hung on and managed to keep it from crashing into the opposing bank.

Fowler was lucky. It was dawn and there was no traffic to broadside him. He was lucky too that the Ford's engine didn't stall. He ran up the berm for a few seconds and maneuvered the truck back into the westbound lane.

The truck was running, but it was tilted askew by a broken spring. The frame was likely bent, and it would strain the transmission and differential. He was miles from the Summit, but if his luck held, he might still get out of this alive.

Porter pounded his steering wheel in frustration, his front wheels on the edge of the bank. The situation wasn't lost yet. In two more miles, he could take an intersecting road and be back on the highway in short order. Fowler was hurt and he didn't know his way around the mountain. Odds were good he'd stay on Route 40. If he could catch Fowler, Porter could still salvage the situation.

Fowler drove as fast as he could and still control the lopsided truck. Thirty-five miles per hour was about the top speed he could hope for. His head pounded with every heart beat, and he felt at times that he might black out. He kept a wary eye on his rearview mirror. So far there was no sign of Porter. He could have abandoned the truck, but he was in no shape to walk anywhere.

The ridges made the road a roller coaster. To spare the transmission, he held in the clutch and let the truck coast downhill. Gravity did its work, but the truck picked up speed each time and Fowler had to use his brakes to keep it under control.

If Porter did catch him, Fowler still had the shotgun. Remingtons held three shells. Fowler fired two at Porter during the escape, which left him one shell in the pipe. If Jumbo's man had a shell in the chamber, two.

The shotgun lay on the floor of the cab, just out of reach. He took his foot off the gas for a second and stretched to put it on the gun. He dragged it close enough to reach with his hand and pulled it onto the seat beside him.

A roadside sign read MOUNT SUMMIT INN DINING AND ACCOMMODATIONS in bold letters and below it, ONE MILE. Almost there. In his suitcase were backup guns and ammunition. And in the room was a phone. One more mile.

He was climbing the last uphill grade to the crest of the mountain when Porter pulled alongside, aiming his pistol at Fowler's head.

Fowler had training in evasive driving, but techniques that worked well in an ordinary car didn't translate well to a crippled truck. Fowler tapped the brake, and Porter's shot went wide, shattering the passenger window.

Fowler waited for Porter to pull alongside again and swung the shotgun into the window. He fired, but at the last second Porter cracked the gas and the coupe shot forward. Buckshot peppered the rear fender of Porter's coupe but missed the tire.

They were almost to the crest and the entrance to the hotel when a car shot over the hill in the other direction head on in Porter's lane. Porter swerved onto the berm, barely missing the oncoming car and nearly crashing into the high bank beyond it.

Fowler missed the hotel entrance and now was rolling down the three mile downhill stretch. He remembered Calvin's words: "burned his brakes out on the grade." The truck was new, but there was no guarantee how the brakes would hold if he got rolling too fast. To his right, the mountain rose sharply. To his left beyond the pavement and a post-and-cable guardrail, it fell away as sharply into a mass of thirty foot trees, their tops at eye level.

Porter was still on his tail. Fowler stood on his brake, and Porter's car ran into the back of the truck. Fowler was hoping for radiator damage or worse. No such luck. Porter was still coming. They were on a broad curve to the right when Porter pulled alongside again, pistol blazing.

One shot left. Maybe.

Fowler aimed the shotgun, not at Porter but at his right front tire. He pulled the trigger, and the shotgun roared. Porter's tire blew out. Fowler wrenched the steering wheel hard left, pushing the coupe across the oncoming lane and the berm, through the guardrail, and over the edge to plunge into the ravine below.

Fowler spun the wheel to the right, nearly going over the edge himself and maneuvered the truck back onto the pavement into the path of a car climbing the mountain. He wrenched the wheel hard left, slewing the truck out of its path, but the maneuver cost him in control.

He fought to turn away from the rise beyond the berm, but his front wheel climbed the steep slope, flipping the truck on its side. It skidded a good fifty feet with a banshee shriek of metal on concrete and came to rest halfway in the westbound lane.

Fowler lay, nearly unconscious in the cab. Gasoline. He smelled gasoline. He braced himself and kicked at the windshield. He heard the crackle of flames behind him. On the third try, the glass gave and he was halfway through the opening when he heard voices.

"There he is! Get him out before it blows!"

Strong hands grabbed his arms and shoulders, pulling him free and dragging him away from the truck. There was a whump and Fowler felt the blast of heat on his face as the gas tank exploded in a ball of fire.

"What?" a man said, leaning over Fowler. "What did you say?"

"FBI. Call the FBI." Fowler mumbled and slipped into blackness.

(14)

Voices. Fowler opened his eyes and saw a white ceiling with a glass light fixture. He turned his head and saw Larry and Sally sitting in chairs across the room.

"He's awake," Sally said.

She stepped to the side of his bed.

"Hi." he said weakly. He tried to reach for her but his arm wouldn't move. He looked down and saw it was encased in a plaster cast.

"Hi, yourself." Her smile was as weak as Fowler's voice. "You never do anything halfway, do you, Dan?"

"What fun would that be?" He coughed and winced at the pain in his head. "What time is it?"

"You mean what day is it. It's Wednesday." Kendall said. "You've been out for two days."

Fowler tried to rise from the mattress but fell back. "I have to get out of this bed. The case . . . ." His voice trailed off.

"Do you want to tell him, or shall I?" Kendall said.

"You were there. Go ahead."

"What?" Fowler said, "What happened?"

"When you didn't check in, Sally stepped over the protocol and initiated a search. You weren't at your hotel, and a call to Treasury told us that Porter was missing too. That got things moving full tilt. I contacted the Pennsylvania State Police, and when they told me a John Doe was involved in a spectacular crash on the mountain, I knew it had to be you."

"It was McCain killing the agents," Fowler blurted. "And Porter —Porter was working for him."

"We figured that out. When the State Police I.D.'d Porter dead in his car at the bottom of a ravine and the truck you were driving as belonging to Jumbo McCain, it was pretty obvious. Witnesses to the crash and the chase that led up to it said there was gunfire. Like I said, obvious."

"And we found you here," Sally said. "But you had no credentials. Because you were Driving McCain's truck, The State Police thought you were part of his crew and Porter was chasing you when you killed him."

"They got the last part right."

"They had you cuffed to the bed 'til we identified you as a Federal agent."

"Is the Bureau going after McCain?"

"The Director was furious. He pulled out all the stops," Sally said. "He sent every available agent."

"Including you?" Fowler said.

"Including me. We descended on McCain's farm en masse. Tell him what we found, Larry."

"There was one hell of a gunfight in the barn before we got there. They were all dead, McCain and his whole crew."

"Who did it?"

"It wasn't a rival family. We dug .45 caliber rounds out of the walls. Hillbillies don't use Tommy guns."

"It looks as if Jumbo McCain crossed some people meaner than himself."

"By the way, we found your badge in the barn," Sally said, "and these."

She put a pair of automatics on the bed beside him. "The serial numbers match. They're yours."

The doctor came in. "You folks are going to have to leave. This man needs rest."

"Okay, Doc," Larry said. "Get well, Dan. Director's orders. You can fill in the blanks tomorrow."

"Don't look, Larry." Sally bent over Fowler and tenderly kissed his lips.

Kendall chuckled. "Didn't see a thing."

(15)

Three days later, Fowler was back in the office where he was debriefed. A heap of paperwork was waiting on his desk. Fowler was plowing through it when his phone rang.

"Fowler."

"The Director wants to see you."

"Now," Fowler said to himself. He stood and put his right arm into his suit jacket and draped it over his injured arm.

The Director's secretary waved him in, where he found Himself, hands clasped behind his back, looking through his window to the street below. "Sit down, Agent Fowler."

The Director sat on the command side of the desk, and Fowler sat in one of the Inquisition chairs. "I read the field account of the investigation. Quite an adventure you had in the hinterlands."

"Yes, sir."

"I am recommending you for a commendation. Your adaptability in the face of adversity is nothing short of remarkable."

"Thank you, sir."

"McCain's demise leaves a vacuum, and I expect that there will be blood over it until either the Brickers or the Headleys emerge the winner."

"Can it be stopped?"

The Director shook his head. "To succeed would mean the reversal of nearly two centuries of tradition, of a whole way of life for a people who want nothing more than to live like their grandfathers and their grandfathers before them. Do you know the myth of Sisyphus, Agent Fowler?"

"I do. He was condemned to the Underworld where he perpetually rolled a boulder up a hill, and when he neared the crest, it rolled back down, and he had to begin again."

"Yes. I see the same futility and frustration inherent in dealing with the Moonshiners. Break up one still, and another will be running the next day. Break up one ring, and another will replace it overnight. Like bailing out the ocean with a bucket. I pity Treasury the task."

The Director looked at his watch, and at almost the same instant, his phone rang. He picked it up, listened a moment, and said, "Send him in."

The door opened, and Keogh stepped into the room.

Fowler leaped to his feet. He snarled, "You bastard, sending me blind into that snake pit." He balled his right hand into a fist and took a step toward him. "I oughta –"

"Agent Fowler!" The Director's voice was like a gunshot. He rose from his chair and came around the desk to stand between them. "That's not how my agents behave." He turned to Keogh and punched him square in the mouth.

Keogh tumbled backward over a chair. Before he could stand up, the Director stood over him. "Who the hell do you think you are, putting one of my agents in that kind of peril with no warning? You go back to Morgenthau and tell him the Bureau is through cleaning up his messes. Never again, and I don't care if the President requests it. Now get out, and don't you ever set foot in this building again."

Keogh rose to a half crouch and scuttled crabwise out the door. The Director closed it and returned to his chair.

Fowler stared at the Director, incredulous.

"That was eminently satisfying," the Director said. "I wanted you to see that, Fowler, and know that there is some justice in this world. I used to take great comfort when I was younger, knowing if all else failed, I could climb over the desk and punch the son of a bitch in the teeth. I can't do that anymore. Now that I'm older, I have to walk around it."

"Thank you, sir," Fowler said, and he meant it.

"I want you to take two weeks leave to put yourself back in working shape."

"With all due respect, sir, I had hoped to get back to work on the Herbertson case."

"And you may, Agent Fowler, in two weeks." The Director opened his desk drawer, pulled out a file and began reading it.

Dismissed.

Downstairs, Fowler stopped by Sally's desk. She beamed when she saw him. "What's up, Dan?"

"The Director said to take two weeks off."

"Oh yeah? What are your plans?"

"Before I answer that question, tell me, do you have any vacation time coming?"

"I might. Why?"

"There's this great hotel I found in Pennsylvania . . . ."

THE END

AFTERWORD:

Fayette County, Pennsylvania has enjoyed its reputation as the Commonwealth's Moonshine Capital ever since Hopwood resident John Gaddis fomented the Whiskey Rebellion in 1794. To this day, stills can be found cooking mash in the forests of the Allegheny Mountains, part of the Appalachian chain, in remote places with names like Hammet's Mountain, Kasparis, and Mount Braddock.

I remember hearing stories as a boy of "Revenuers" going into the forest in search of stills and never being seen again, which inspired this story.

Demand for the potent corn liquor among the locals hasn't ebbed in two centuries, and although local distilleries now produce it legally, and many "entrepreneurs" now grow Marijuana and cook crystal meth in the woods instead, moonshine still flows from the wilds of Fayette County.

Before the e-mails start, I realize that the FBI had no official female agents until the 1960s. Please indulge my Artist's License in making Sally Vane an agent, for the sake of a good story.

ABOUT OUR CREATORS

WRITER -

FRED ADAMS, JR. is a retired English instructor from Penn State University who has spent a lifetime enjoying what his colleagues jokingly called his "literary slumming," reading pulp fiction. Now that he's off the clock, he's expanded that pursuit, writing pulp novels, more than twenty since 2014. Many have been published by Airship 27 Productions, beginning with *Hitwolf* in that year and the most recent being the vampire/pirate novel *Fangs of the Sea*. Others include the Six Gun Terrors series, the Ike Mars series, and the C.O. Jones series plus others and a spate of short stories for Airship 27 anthologies..

He currently resides in Mount Pleasant, Pennsylvania where, as he is fond of saying, he lives "in perpetual terror of boredom."

INTERIOR ILLUSTRATIONS –

SAM A. SALAS - has a been an artist since the 70's. His first love has always been comics and comic book art. His greatest aspiration was to become a comic book artist with one of the major companies. In the mid 90's Sam and a small band of friends decided to publish his own comics. Thus was born ZUB COMICS. The company published two titles. One was GREAT GALAXIES! A science fiction anthology featuring all original stories with art by Sam. The other title was TELLURIA a fantasy title. In all, the company published 11 books and folded in the early 2000's.

Since then, Sam has done various freelance projects for local independent publishers including several stories for a book titled WICKED AWESOME TALES, and a few stories for Ron Fortier. Now mostly retired, he is always ready to take on new projects and looks forward to working with his friend Ron on this new book.

COVER ARTIST -

MICHAEL YOUNGBLOOD —Of Asheville N.C. has a bachelor's degree in art and has done most of his work in architectural illustration and design. He's also done various other freelance projects since 1991.